'On this dunghill we will search among the rubble for our talisman of hope'
This Earth, My Brother, Kofi Awoonor

TAIL OF THE BLUE BIRD

Nii Ayikwei Parkes

Tail of the
Blue Bird

Jonathan Cape
London

Published by Jonathan Cape 2009

2 4 6 8 10 9 7 5 3 1

Copyright © Nii Ayikwei Parkes 2009

Nii Ayikwei Parkes has asserted his right under the Copyright,
Designs and Patents Act 1988 to be identified as the author of this work

First published in Great Britain in 2009 by
Jonathan Cape
Random House, 20 Vauxhall Bridge Road,
London SW1V 2SA

www.rbooks.co.uk

Addresses for companies within The Random House Group Limited can be found at:
www.randomhouse.co.uk/offices.htm

The Random House Group Limited Reg. No. 954009

A CIP catalogue record for this book
is available from the British Library

ISBN 9780224085748

The Random House Group Limited supports the Forest Stewardship
Council (FSC), the leading international forest certification organisation. All our titles that are
printed on Greenpeace-approved FSC certified paper carry the FSC logo. Our paper
procurement policy can be found at www.rbooks.co.uk/environment

Mixed Sources
Product group from well-managed
forests and other controlled sources
www.fsc.org Cert no. TT-COC-2139
© 1996 Forest Stewardship Council
FSC

Typeset by Palimpsest Book Production Limited,
Grangemouth, Stirlingshire
Printed and bound in Great Britain by
Printed in the UK by CPI Mackays, Chatham, ME5 8TD

kwasida – nkyi kwasi

THE BIRDS HAVE NEVER STOPPED SINGING. IF YOU LOOK YOU will see that whatever happens the birds will sing their song. In my grandfather's time the forest was thick thick and higher; we didn't have to go far to kill a hog. Ah, their spoor began at the edge of the village and the taste of boar meat was like water to us, we ate so much. I remember well. Now they have gone deep deep, the boar. But all things are in Onyame's wide hands. Only Onyame, the shining one, knows why a goat's shit is so beautiful. We are not complaining. When I go to forest I can see that the world is wonderful. The birds are all colours colours. Red, sea blue, yellow, some like leaves, some white like fresh calico. What creatures can you not find there? The smallest catch I have ever brought home is adanko. (Ndanko are not hard to catch. Even when they hide, their ears stick up so you can see them. If I created them I would have put their eyes on their pointed ears to keep them safe, but then I wouldn't be able to catch them. Maybe hunger would consume me. Ah, ndanko. They are fast, but I have many traps. That is a hunter's life.)

So we are not complaining. The village is good. We are close to the chief's village and we can take any matters to him. But we have just twelve families so we have no trouble. Apart from Kofi Atta. He is my relative, but before I learned how to wear cloth my mother told me that he would bring heavy matters to us. I remember; my father had brought otwe – *antelope* – the night before and she was cooking abenkwan.

Yaw Poku, she said, when you are playing with your relative look well ooh.

Yoo.

Yaw Poku! (My mother said things to me twice.) I said look well when you play with Kofi Atta. You hear?

Yoo.

She took my hand and put hot soup in it for me to taste. Then she said, You don't know that the woman who helped his mother lost his umbilical cord? She shook her head. It is not buried. The boy will bring trouble someday.

So maybe I shouldn't be surprised, but I forgot. We don't think of these things. They are like light. In the day there is always light and we don't think about it, but I, Yaw Poku, am a hunter so light surprises me. I am used to the dimness of forest, the way the light falls on me like incisions from a knife when I move. When I go to forest sound is brighter than light, so light surprises me. The same way I was surprised even though my mother warned me to look well – *be careful.*

We were at our somewhere when they came. First it was the young woman whose eyes could not rest. Hmm, since you are here let me tell you. The ancestors say that the truth is short but, sɛbi, when the tale is bad, then even the truth stretches like a toad run over by a car on those new roads they are building. I, the one who crouches, the one who watches, I, Yaw Poku who has roamed the forests from Atewa to Kade, seen every duiker, hog, cobra and leopard that turns this our earth, I was surprised. But let me tell you the tale before it goes cold. It was my grandfather, Opoku, the one whose hands were never empty, who told me that the tale the English man calls *history* is mostly lies written in fine dye. This is no such

2

tale. It is said that the wise weaver of webs, Ananse, did not sell speech, so I shall speak. I shall tell the tale.

It was kwasida, nkyi kwasi – just *one week* before kuru-kwasi, when it would be a taboo, sɛbi, to speak of death and funerals. Nawotwe before we were to pour libation for the ones on the other side. I am sure of the day but if you think I'm lying you can check with the Bono, who have kept the days for the Asantehene for centuries.

We were at our somewhere when she came. The one whose eyes would not lie still. I myself was coming from the palm-wine tapper's hut. (The woman who sells palm wine doesn't open on kwasida. She went to live in the big city, Accra, for six years and when she came back she refused to work on *Sundays*. Before she went to the city she used to sell tomatoes at the roadside, but that is another story.) The palm-wine tapper gave me a large calabash of his *special* and I was going back to my hut when I heard the woman scream like a grass-cutter in a trap. I don't play with my palm wine, no, no, so I went to put it in the corner of my hut, then I came to the tweneboa tree in the village centre.

She was wearing these short short skirts some. Showing her thighs, sɛbi, but her legs were like a baby otwe's front two legs – thiiiin. (It was later that I found out she was some *minister's* girlfriend. Hmm. This world is full of wonders.) Her *driver* was wearing *khaki* up and down like a colo man and he wanted to hold her still, but the woman was shaking her head and screaming. And there she strengthened herself and ran towards a pale car at the roadside. The *driver* followed her rear like dust.

When I asked the children, Oforiwaa, Kusi and the twins – Panyin and Kakra, who were playing in the village centre – what happened, they said the *cream Benz* parked and the woman was

3

following a blue-headed bird (it is true that our village has many beautiful things) when she held her nose. She called her *driver* and they sniffed the air like dogs until they got to Kofi Atta's hut. They said Agoo, but nobody answered. Then the *driver* raised the kɛtɛ and held it up and the woman went inside. That's when she screamed. It was still morning and the sound made the forest go quiet. But it's what happened after they left that's wondrous. It is true. Even the eagle has not seen everything.

The sun was at its highest, sitting hard in the middle of the sky. I was resting on the felled palm by the tweneboa tree, listening to my *radio* (these days I catch this new *Sunrise FM* from Koforidua), drinking some of my palm wine and watching the children play when they came. The first car came towards the tree at top speed and screeched to a stop, raising sand like rice husks. There were two aburuburu in the trees. I'm telling you, they flew off, making that sound like pouring water in their throats and flapping wildly as the other cars stopped near the first. There were five cars in all. *Police* cars. The first car wasn't even like the *police* cars you sometimes see. It was a *Pinzgauer* with a long *aerial* on top; that's how I knew it was a big matter. *Pinzgauers* are what the army use when they go into jungle for training; I have seen them while hunting.

The big man in *mufti* got down from the *Pinzgauer*. He was wearing a big black abomu over his *jeans* and he was eating groundnuts.

Who is in charge here?

The children pointed towards the giant kapok tree beyond Asare's farm. *The chief lives in that village there.*

The other *policemen* had come down from their cars, all in black black. *Policemen* one, one – nine, in our village on this young day. The one in *mufti* looked left and right, then I saw him looking behind the tree at my mother's blue sanyaa basin that I put on top of my hut after she died. I remember she carried water with it until it was full of holes, then she took it to her farm to harvest vegetables until there was just a big hole at the bottom. I put it on top of the grass on my roof so I can see my house from far when I am coming back from forest. When the *policeman* looked, I looked too. And there he looked at me and pointed.

You, do you speak English?

Ah. I thought this man either doesn't respect or because, sεbi, I have shaved my hair he can't see my seventy-four years. Chewing groundnuts while speaking to me! I didn't say anything. I raised my calabash and drank some of Kwaku Wusu's palm wine. It was good. Kwaku Wusu is the best tapper in the sixteen villages under our chief and the twelve villages under Nana Afari.

You. The *policeman* walked towards me, while the children jumped around him. Oforiwaa started singing a Papa *Police* song (that girl is always singing) and clapping. Kusi was standing by the eight *policemen* in uniform, touching their guns while they tried to push him away. These *policemen*, they carry guns all the time, everywhere. Even I, a hunter, I put my long gun down on kwasida.

His name is Opanyin Poku, said the twins.

Ah, said the *policeman, senior man.* He showed his mother's training and swallowed his groundnuts and put his hands behind him. Opanyin Poku, please, do you speak English?

I smiled and finished my palm wine. Small, small. I go for Nkrumah adult education.

OK, listen. I no get plenty time. I dey house for Accra wey I get call say some woman find something for here wey e dey smell. You know something for the matter?

Ei, the elders say that news is as restless as a bird, but as for

5

this! The woman had come in the morning and it was still morning, afternoon had not yet come, but these *policemen* were here all the way from Accra, as if there were no *policemen* in Tafo. I shook my head.

You see the woman?

Oh yes *police*, I see am. Thiiin woman like so.

The *policeman* smiled. But you no dey smell anything?

No, I no dey smell anything.

Ah, ah. He turned to look at the other *policemen*. *Do you people smell anything?*

Yes Sergeant, it stinks like rotten meat.

Thank you. He turned to me again. And you no dey smell anything?

No, Sargie.

He shook his head. So where the woman go?

Accra.

No. Which side she go for here? He raised his arm towards the tweneboa tree.

I pointed at Kofi Atta's hut.

He brought his hand down to hold the black stick in his abomu. *Let's go.*

The other *policemen* followed him. After a little distance he stopped and turned to me. Opanyin Poku, I beg, make you come some.

I called Kusi to come and get my calabash and radio, put them at the door of my house and tell Mama Aku that I'll be back later. Then I stood up and walked to join the *policemen*.

The sargie was trying to send the other children back but they were still singing and refused to leave. He looked at me.

Children, I said. Stop your silliness and go home.

They stopped following the *policemen* and turned to leave. Suddenly the sargie clapped. *Children, do you smell anything? No sir, Sergeant.* They laughed and ran off.

6

The sargie frowned and looked at me. Opanyin Poku, why say we all dey smell something wey you people for here no dey smell anything?

I laughed. Sargie, make I talk something for Twi inside?

Oh, Opanyin, no problem.

Then listen Sargie. Sɛbi, our village is like a vagina. Those on the inside have no problems with it; those on the outside think it stinks.

*

The mouth of Kofi Atta's hut was untidy. There was a heap of bidie near his fireplace and a broken water pot by the door. The obsidian from the water pot was lying under the kɛtɛ like the lost eye of a giant bat. The sargie and the other *policemen* held their noses and looked at each other. I could see they were scared. Sargie pointed at the kɛtɛ and the tall red *policeman* raised it. I went inside and all the *policemen* one, one – nine came inside. None of them thought of holding the kɛtɛ so the sun could come in. As for me, I didn't care. It was dark but I could see. The was a little space in the grass in Kofi Atta's roof so some flimsy sun was able to squeeze through like the deep deep forest. I could smell old palm wine. (Kofi Atta liked to store his palm wine until it became bitter and strong.) There was something on Kofi Atta's kɛtɛ, about the size of a newborn otwe.

Kai, Sargie shouted, *it stinks in here*. He took a *flashlight* out of his abomu and switched it on.

And there, all the *policemen* started shouting. Oh Awurade! Ei Yesu! Asɛm bɛn ni! which would have made me laugh because they were all speaking English before that, but it's true that what we saw . . . it's not something you see every day. Even I, Yaw Poku. And when fear catches you, it returns you to screaming, your first language.

The thing lying on Kofi Atta's kɛtɛ was quivering. It was

7

black and shiny, but when the tall red *policeman* stepped closer it was wansima, about apem apem, *thousands*. They took off and the hut was filled with their buzzing. I ran towards the wall, but they surrounded the *policemen*, who stamped around trying to brush them off. I turned and removed the cloth from Kofi Atta's window-hole and all the wansima left, except for one or two that kept hovering around. The sun entered the room and we all saw what was on the kɛtɛ. It looked like, sɛbi, a skinned adanko, but it had no bones and it was red red, like a woman's monthly troubles.

It's a dead baby, said the tall red *policeman*.

Sargie shook his head.

Another, dark, but not dark dark, with a gap between his teeth, said: *This is not natural*.

Sargie stepped back and put his hands in the back pockets of his *jeans*. *All right officers, let us not forget our duties*. Mensah?

The tall red one turned to him. *Sir?*

Cordon off this abode. He turned to me. Opanyin Poku weytin you know about this thing?

Nothing Sargie, I told him. Because truly I was shocked. I was not meant to see what I saw, sɛbi. No one without the right powers was supposed to see it. I knew I had to pour libation as soon as possible. All this because of some woman in a short short skirt with thin legs. Ah, the elders did not lie when they said one palm nut spoils the enjoyment of the palm wine. I walked out of Kofi Atta's hut and stood outside holding my head.

Sargie came outside with all the *policemen*, leaving the tall red one inside. He took a *radio* from his abomu and pushed something, then he spoke:

Inspector Donkor, Sergeant Mintah reporting. We suspect human remains, sir . . . We are not sure . . . With respect, we can't be sure, sir. We are not qualified . . . Sorry, sir. Yes, sir, we will try harder . . . Of course, sir. We can get a pathologist. We'll try

Koforidua . . . Sir, we will begin interrogation shortly . . . Yes sir. Yes sir. I'll update you, sir.

When he finished talking he turned to the men. *All right, I want you to split into three groups of two and question everyone, adult, man, woman and child, in this village.* Mensah, *I want you to guard this hut.* Gavu, *wait here.*

The one with the gap between his teeth said *Yes, sir,* and the rest went towards the centre of the village.

Sargie put his hand in the pocket of his shirt, removed some groundnuts and started chewing. He turned to me. *Yaw Poku, you say you don't know anything about this?*

I looked at him. This young man who had left his training at home, who was calling me Yaw Poku, who had forgotten that I was helping him. Now he wanted to be a big *officer* so he was speaking to me in English. I wanted to tell him that you do not light a fire under a fruit-bearing tree, but these young people think they invented knowledge so I ignored him.

Do you know who lives here?

He's called Kofi Atta. I started walking away.

Sargie chased me. *Where are you going?*

To pour libation.

He laughed and waved towards the mouth of Kofi Atta's hut. Gavu, *let's move. We're going to Koforidua.*

As I reached the tweneboa tree I saw one of the *policemen* shaking Asare, the farmer, with his wife and the children watching. These people: *policemen. lawyers, ministers,* they will never learn; book law and gun power can never teach you how to deal with human beings. We have always had our own ways; remember that the monkey was eating long before the farmer was born. I shook my head and went to get my palm wine.

*

By the time Sargie came back we were all angry. We had gathered around the tweneboa tree and we refused to answer any of the questions the *policemen* asked. All of us except the three boys who now live in forest and Oduro, who was with them, watching us from the two prɛkɛsɛ trees near Asare's farm. It was Gawana who suggested that we gather around the tweneboa tree. He said: 'They are not many; they can't force us.' Truly, he made me happy paa. He will do well that boy. He is in school in Kumasi but he was on holiday. You see, even a *schoolboy* like him, he didn't try to speak big English. Gawana is a good boy. He is not really from this village but he is one of us. I've told him he could be a good hunter.

His grandfather came here in '54. He said he came all the way from *Kenya*, walking, and jumping on *trucks* when he had the chance. Kojo Sei translated for him but we didn't believe any of it. Kojo Sei was known for his stories. The thing was, Gawana was so good-looking, with smooth dark skin, a long head and big eyes. So good-looking that one of the women – my sister's husband's mother's sister's daughter, Ama Serwaa – fell in love with him. (You know, our women can choose their men as long as their parents agree. Marriage is a family matter.) When he learned Twi he told us that the English man was cutting off their testicles in *Kenya* so he ran. At first we laughed. Sɛbi, what man cuts off another man's testicles? But he showed us marks on his back where he had been beaten in the street and we started to believe him. We never really asked his name, but we heard Ama Serwaa calling him Gawana. After that we called all his family Gawana. Big Gawana, little Gawana, girl Gawana, boy Gawana and now this young Gawana was one of us. Speaking Twi like the chief's own son. Standing in front of these *policemen* and telling them to stop *harassing* us. Ah, the ancestors knew what they were talking about when they said Abusua yɛ dom. If your family won't fight for you, who will? The family is indeed an army.

*

10

The man Sargie brought, the *pathologis*, was drunk. I could tell by the looseness of his eyes. (I'm a regular at the palmwine hut, so I know drink.) When Sargie found that his men had unearthed no matters from us to tell him, he shouted at them and called them *incompetent*. He told them to go and sit in their cars, then he went towards Kofi Atta's hut with the *pathologis* and the *policeman* with the gap in his teeth. The village people began to go home. My wife, Aku, was with them, but, you know me, I stayed by the tree to watch. The tall red *policeman* was still standing at Kofi Atta's door with a long gun on his shoulder, just like that.

When they came back out Sargie was frowning and asking the *pathologis* questions. *So you can't say for sure what it is?*

No. I deal with dead people. That is not a dead person.

Then what is it?

It could be anything. My guess would be afterbirth, but it seems a little big for that. He coughed and spat on the ground. He wasn't a healthy man; his spit was the colour of a crushed grasshopper.

You are sure it's not a dead person?

Officer, it has no bones. People have bones.

Sargie nodded. *Excuse me, Doctor*, he said. Then he removed his *radio*, pressed the thing again and started talking:

Inspector Donkor, it's me . . . Yes, sir, he's here . . . . He says possibly afterbirth . . . No, sir, he's not sure . . . Sir, with respect, it is almost night now and there is no evidence of foul play. Why can't we just drop the case? . . . I beg your pardon, sir. I'm sorry . . . Sorry sir. I am not questioning your judgement. Inspector Donkor, I'm very sorry . . . Yes, I am aware that was the minister's girlfriend . . . I trust you, sir. We shall carry on . . . Oh, the graduate? I don't remember his name, sir. I never met him. It was DI Baah who interviewed him . . . I'll try, sir. See you in Accra, sir.

He put the *radio* back in his abomu and walked towards the tweneboa tree. The *pathologis* followed him with an unsteady walk.

OK. Sargie patted the top of the car at the back. *Take the doctor back to his drinking cronies in Koforidua and report at Ring Road tomorrow morning. The rest of you, direct to Accra; no curve, no bend.* He signalled the tall red one, who came running.

It was getting dark. We have no *electricity*, and the sun was red behind my hut. I knew by then my wife would be waiting for me. The *police* cars started and the children came running out to watch them leave. Oforiwaa started her Papa *Police* song again.

Mensah, Sargie said, *you will have to stay here tonight to guard the investigation scene.*

Yes, Sergeant.

I know this is a useless case with all these nobodies, but because it's the minister's girlfriend we have to do our best. The inspector thinks he knows someone who can help solve the case. When he comes tomorrow you can come back to Accra.

Yes, Sergeant. He hesitated. *Sergeant,* he said, scratching his head, *no allowance?*

Sargie put his hand in his back pocket and took out many notes. He took six *5,000* notes and passed them to the tall red *policeman.* And there he turned and walked towards the *Pinzgauer.* The *policeman* with the gap in his teeth was now sitting in the driver's seat. He leaned out of the window and asked Sargie: *Who is this person the Inspector is bringing tomorrow?*

Some graduate. Sargie put his hand in his pocket and took some groundnuts. *I still can't believe this fine place stinks so much.* They both laughed. And there, Sargie sat down and they started the *Pinzgauer.* Sargie didn't even look at me when they were leaving. (Ei, what has happened to our people?)

We were at our somewhere when they came; first the woman and her *driver*, then one, one – nine *policemen*, then a drunk *pathologis*. And now they had left us with one tall red *policeman*, a Ga man, I think, and a *police* car that the children climbed in the evening. And they said the next day a *graduate* was coming. (I had to tell the chief in the morning.) We waited to see. Man has his plans and the ancestors also have their plans, and sometimes they are not the same. The needs of the earth are greater than the needs of us. We are not complaining. My father and his father before him were hunters; that is what was chosen. My own two sons have not followed me; they have gone to their mother's family in the south. So I am the last hunter in this village. I have seen all the wonders of the forests and rivers and I have told many of the young men, but they all want to go to the cities and make money. Even the story of how I followed the Densu river; rode it in a dugout canoe learning the birds' songs as the current carried me down, watched the many-patterned butterflies flutter on the river-banks, ran my hand in the water like a fish swimming all the way down to the mangroves of the south, where I saw my wife bathing naked in the waters; her buttocks wide and dark, her legs strong and bowed, her beauty greater than a royal python's. Even that story does not entice them. They say there are beautiful women everywhere now. And I tell them that it is not just about beauty because beauty doesn't pay debts. But do they listen?

The medicine man, Oduro, can't find an assistant, and the young ones don't trust him anymore; they want *tablets* and he gives them leaves.

Things are not the same. But night had fallen just the same.

I had been out too long and it was time to go to my wife. That red *policeman* was smoking something. I could smell it. If he wanted to stay awake he should have chewed cola; smoke does not keep the eyes open. (Oh, Kofi Atta! Because of you all these people have come to do what they like in our village.) My eyes had seen what the mouth must not speak, but one must not let the sight of death, sebi, stop one from sleeping, and so I went home. Those who have lived know that darkness is only temporary; morning brings its own light.

dwowda

THE RADIO WAS PLAYING THAT SONG AGAIN, ADUU SUMO Akwadu, monkey loves banana. Kayo didn't understand why the technicians had to play it so loudly in the lab, but he felt he couldn't say anything because he had told them it was OK to play the radio as long as it didn't affect their output. The work they did was analysing sample after sample of agricultural chemicals, food ingredients and flavourings, human and animal fluids, new products for importers wanting to prove that they met the requirements set by the Ghana Standards Board for whatever they were selling, and recently, water samples for all these *pure water* companies sprouting up everywhere. It sounded interesting, in the same way that sports highlights sounded so on the radio. But the listener is never there when the athletes, boxers, gymnasts, cricketers and footballers have to wake up at 4 a.m. to train, to run up the same hill a hundred times until the echo of the earth beneath their feet begins to haunt them. In the minutiae even the most colourful skirt is just fabric, strips of cotton, men and women sat around a loom in Egypt bored out of their heads. Biochemical analysis was the same. Even he found it boring, and he at least had the computer and could play *Minesweeper* while pretending to schedule their work.

Kayo got up from his desk and shut the door that led to the main lab. To keep his reputation as a good manager he had to quell his anger sometimes. With his door shut he could still hear strains of the song, its jiggling syncopations, but he couldn't hear the lyrics. He dropped back into his seat, rolled back on the black plastic wheels, and placed his feet on the desk. He was frustrated that they seemed to enjoy the song so much no matter how many times an hour the radio stations played it. In fact, they seemed to be happy with everything; even the fact that they were all overqualified for their jobs and had an egomaniac like Mr Acquah for a boss. That was the problem with this country. People were being manipulated and exploited but they continued to sing. The song was like the system; it gave no new information – the whole world knows that monkeys love bananas – no new solutions, but everyone hailed it as the best thing ever. He shook his head and closed his eyes.

His life was giving him headaches. Working in a biochemical lab was not what he wanted to be doing and after eleven months it was beginning to wear him thin. He had thought it would only be for four months, until he secured a role with the police. He hadn't counted on the slow grind of the public institutions, the number of weeks it would take for him to get a simple application form. He had all but given up. This office was now his life. This wide white-framed window overlooking seven workers in a lab dancing to melodies he could no longer stand. The polished granite floor represented failure to him; the grey filing cabinet was an eavesdropper tittering at his bad luck, the telephone a shrill-voiced aunt mocking him.

Of course Mr Acquah was pleased to have Kayo on his staff. He was practically salivating when Kayo arrived for an interview.

Mr Acquah's office was completely wrong for a bio institution; the meat-red carpet was a perfect breeding ground for microorganisms. But Kayo said nothing. He needed to work. His meagre savings from England were emergency money. For now he wanted an income so he could help pay his sister's way through university. His parents had poured everything they had into his education and now it was payback time; it was never said, but it was expected. His sister first, then his brother.

'So, you are a forensic pathologist.' Mr Acquah's tone indicated this was a question.

'Yes.'

'This means you are a doctor, you can do advanced medical analysis and diagnosis.' The excitement in Mr Acquah's voice was making him rasp. Again it was a question. Kayo would later find out that his joining the laboratory had literally doubled their business.

'Yes, I can do exactly what my CV says I can do.' Kayo's voice rose slightly and he stared squarely at the rotund man trapped in a pristine white lab coat with his name clearly marked above the left pocket. The state of the coat told Kayo that Mr Acquah rarely set foot in the actual laboratory; he probably held court in his plush office, looking like a white mouse on parade.

'You're quite tall.'

'Excuse me?' Kayo instinctively tilted his head to the right.

'I said you're quite tall. Most people who work in labs are short.'

Kayo shook his head, took his feet off the table and sat up. It was only 10:03 a.m. and he was already looking forward to having a drink after work. His social life was the only thing that kept him sane. With his friends he could rant at the system and feel better. His best friend Nii Nortey laughed with him, but in private he advised Kayo that if he really wanted to work for the police he needed to identify the right people in the force and bribe them.

Kayo found it hard to come to grips with the concept. If he bribed someone to get a job when he was perfectly qualified he would feel they owed him money, yet the same people would go around thinking he owed them gratitude. He didn't think he could work in such a sandstorm of expectations. He knew the system was like that but it wasn't normal to bribe someone and then have to work with them. You bribed someone, got what you wanted and moved on. That was the system Kayo understood; the system that had allowed his father to persuade a clerk to add a year to Kayo's age so he could qualify for a government scholarship when he was still sixteen.

There was a knock at his door.

'Yes, come in.' Through the window, he saw Joseph, the senior biomed lab technician, who poked his head round the door. Kayo waved him in.

'Sir, we're running out—'

'Joseph,' Kayo cut in. 'What did we discuss last week?'

Joseph smiled and looked down. 'That I shouldn't call you "sir".'

'Exactly. You are older than me and you have a family. It's not right.'

'Sorry, Mr Kayo.'

Kayo shook his head, knowing Mr Kayo was the best he would get. 'How can I help?'

'Mr Kayo, we are running out of some of the reagents and basic chemicals. We need urea and trigliceride. Also, sodium hydroxide.'

'OK.' Kayo took out a notepad and jotted down Joseph's requests in chemical abbreviations. 'Is that all?'

'Oh, I think we will soon need more gloves as well, and disposable droppers.'

'Fine.'

Joseph left the door open when leaving. Another radio favourite, 'Philomena', filled the office and Kayo found himself singing along without meaning to. He spotted Joseph coming back.

'Mr Kayo, I forgot. Micro-centrifuge tubes also.' He smiled and turned to leave.

'Joseph.'

'Yes, sir?'

'Please close my door.'

Kayo opened his stock-keeping spreadsheet and frowned. He would have to speak to Mr Acquah about increasing the biomed department's budget. After all, they made more money than any other department. He reached for the green telephone at the edge of his desk and dialled the switchboard.

'Hi, Eunice.'

'Oh hello Kayo, how are you today?' Eunice's voice trilled like a parrot's and it scared him more than the fact that she was on the prowl for what she termed 'a suitable husband' – something that had a lot to do with money and reputation and little to do with attraction. He could imagine the mole on her chin jumping as she spoke. 'Do you want me to order you some food?'

'No.' He shook his head at his filing cabinet; she never waited for him to speak. 'It's only 10:16.'

'Oh, sorry. What can I do for you?'

'Could you please call Sowah Scientific Supplies and put them through when you get them? Their line always seems to be busy when I call.'

'No problem.'

Kayo replaced the receiver in its cradle and made an effort to smile. Enough misery for a day, he decided as he pushed his chair back and stretched his legs. His mother was always reminding him that he was a coast boy from Nyɛmashie, a fisherman; some days the canoes returned with no fish, but it didn't mean that there would not be fish another day. Fishermen had to understand fate and hope. And what was a day anyway? The old ladies in Nyɛmashie had a saying. Kayo frowned.

If you close your eyes there is no night or day. He clicked his fingers and pointed at the ceiling. That's what the old ladies used to say when he was growing up. They would see him running home from the shore, where he spent hours chasing crabs, and ask him why he was rushing.

'It's almost night. My mother will be angry.'

Lifting their heads from the smoked fish they were sorting for sale the next day, the old ladies would wag their fingers.

'She will be worried, but not because of the night.'

Another would chime in, 'Mmm hmm, not because of the night.'

'Then why, Mmaa?' Kayo would ask.

'Because you have been gone a long time.'

'Yes, if you close your eyes there is no night or day, but a mother always misses her child.'

He remembered how upset the women had been when their corner of the country was electrified. They didn't mind the electricity as much as they minded the street lamps. What was the sense in destroying night? They fussed and fussed while the men just watched, hmmphed and mended their nets.

Kayo picked up his phone after the second ring and pulled his pad towards him so he could write while he spoke. It was an old habit. A vestige of his years of writing equations – algebra, physics, chemistry, biochemistry . . . He braced himself for Eunice's voice.

'Kayo?'

'Yes, just put them through.' He didn't understand why she always had to speak to him before she put his calls through.

Eunice hesitated. 'It's not Sowah Scientific, Kayo; they are still ringing engaged. It's one Sergeant Mintah who wants to speak to you.'

'Please put him through.' Kayo wrote *Sergeant* on his pad and waited.

'Hello.'

'Hello.'

'Is that Odamtten?'

'Yes.'

'My name is Sergeant George Mintah. I am calling you on behalf of the PRCC, P. J. Donkor, to assist in an investigation.'

Kayo was momentarily stunned. 'Sorry, are you army or police?'

'Police.'

'OK.' He wrote *Police* on his pad. 'Am I a witness or a suspect?'

The man on the other end laughed so hard that Kayo heard his chair shift. A wooden chair in a hollow room. 'No sah, if you were a suspect we would have been there to arrest you already.'

Kayo exhaled slowly. 'So, how can I help?'

'It seems you are a forensics man and the PRCC has a case he wants your expertise for. Your services are required immediately.'

The irony of the situation brought a smile to Kayo's lips. Less than a year ago the Ghana Police had turned down his job application because, in the words of the red-eyed officer who interviewed him, DI Baah, forensics was 'surplus to requirements'. Yes, he appreciated that Kayo had worked for a year as a scenes of crime officer with the West Midlands Police in England, very admirable, but things were different here. The Ghana Police had a ninety-nine per cent record in solving crimes through 'specialised' interrogation.

Kayo cleared his throat. 'Do you know anything about the case?'

'No sah. But it's not Accra-based. It's in Sonokrom, in the hinterland. Near Tafo.'

'What kind of case is it?'

'The PRCC wrote "unclassified", sah.'

Kayo wrote *Unclassified* on his notepad and drew three arrows leading away from the word in a fan pattern. Under the arrows he wrote: *abduction, theft, murder.* Then he pulled his lower lip and wrote in small boxes: *smuggling, trafficking, fraud.*

'Hello.'

'Yes, Sergeant.'

'So, what should I tell him?'

'I'll have to ask my boss for time off,' said Kayo, tapping his pen against the side of his face. 'I'll call you back.'

'No sah, I'll hold.'

It struck Kayo that there was an element of coercion implicit in the sergeant's insistence on holding. It reminded him of those special-offer adverts where the announcer said the product was only on sale for a few hours; it made you feel as if someone was watching you, waiting to see what you would do. He didn't want to be watched. 'It may take some time,' he said.

'I'll hold.'

Kayo knocked twice on Mr Acquah's door and placed his hand against the grey frame.

'Enter.'

He walked in and stood by one of the two black leather chairs facing Mr Acquah across his pale wood desk. 'Good Morning Mr Acquah.'

'Morning. Sit down.'

Although he was in a hurry, Kayo settled in a chair and placed his palms on the desk. Mr Acquah didn't like it when people stood while he was talking to them. Kayo suspected it was because it made his scattered bald patches stand out. 'Thank you. How are things?'

'Fine. Any problems in the lab?'

'No.'

'You need to borrow some money?'

Kayo smiled.

Mr Acquah seemed to think that anyone who spoke to him for more than two minutes wanted money.

'No, Mr Acquah.' Kayo extended his legs under the desk and accidentally kicked Mr Acquah's shin. 'Sorry.'

Mr Acquah waved a hand impatiently and glanced at his phone. 'Kayo, your mission?'

'Oh, yes, I've been approached by the Ghana Police to help them with some work so I've come to ask if it's possible for me to have some time off.'

Mr Acquah shook his head. 'If the Ghana Police need our services, they must follow procedure; they should speak to me.'

'Mr Acq—'

Mr Acquah thumbed his chest as though he was trying to dislodge the rising rasp in his voice. 'I am the proprietor of this establishment.'

Kayo held a hand over his mouth and sighed. 'Mr Acquah, they need my services as a forensic scientist, and forensics is not one of the services you offer. I'm just asking for a few days.'

Mr Acquah walked to a small fridge in the left corner of his office, extracted a half-drunk bottle of Pepsi, took a swig and replaced it.

Mr Acquah's thrift with the drink reminded Kayo of the first time he had had Pepsi. He was eleven and had just managed to get a scholarship to go to Presbyterian Boys Secondary School. His father brought the bottle home and they all had some – all of them: his mother, his father, his four-year-old sister and two-year-old brother, and himself. And his mother still managed to save some for the next day. Kayo felt a familiar pang of longing as Mr Acquah closed the fridge.

Mr Acquah sat back at his desk. 'Who are you talking to at Ghana Police?'

'Sergeant Mintah.'

'A sergeant? Ah Kayo, you think I'm paying you so that any minnow from nowhere can call you from your job at any time? Have you read your contract?'

'Yes. I know I'm not entitled to any holidays until after twelve months of work. That's why I'm asking you.'

'You read the part about conflict of interest.'

'Mr Acquah, there is no conflict of interest. Forensics is not your business and I am simply asking for a few days.' Kayo clenched his fist beneath the desk to stay calm.

Mr Acquah stood up. 'Ei, my friend, watch your tone.' He pulled up his dark blue trousers and buttoned his lab coat. 'Remember who pays your salary. If you want to speak to me you better humble yourself. Tell Sergeant Whatever to call me and then we'll discuss this matter.'

Kayo glared at Mr Acquah in silence, scrutinising the sheer whiteness of the man's coat. With the contacts Kayo had made in his time with Acquabio, he could, in theory, leave and set up on his own. The problem was that no banks would give him a loan for the equipment. To get a loan of the size he would require you needed to know the right people. Kayo didn't. And even if he did, the interest rates were prohibitive. You could only realistically set up the kind of lab he would need if you had a huge inheritance or some sort of windfall. For the first time Kayo wondered how Mr Acquah had come by his wealth.

'Yes?' Mr Acquah held out two upturned hands like a prophet. In the window behind him, the garden boy, a man in his forties, was bent over a cluster of weeds, digging them out with a hoe, tossing them into a worn basket, and then flattening the black soil tenderly. The man's back was framed by fat green stalks of birds of paradise flowers, all their blooms angled to the sky like miniature orange jets in an air show, except for one, turning dark, drooping with age, a burning fuselage heading for earth. Beyond the flowers Kayo could see a neat wedge of hedges and a curve of the road, with a mild peppering of potholes smothered with loose gravel. Acquabio was tucked away in a corner of North Ridge that gave an impression of calm, but barely held the bustle of Accra at bay. North Ridge was a mysterious collage of embassies, squats, World Bank employee residences, offices and exclusive clubs, but the city whose borders it flirted with was like every one he had been to: a patchwork of dreamers, survivors and mercenaries. The mercenaries lived off the fat of the dreamers and survivors, the survivors' lives were sometimes made easier because of the dreamers, and the dreamers either expired or prospered. Kayo knew that, by nature, he wasn't a mercenary, but he hadn't decided which of the other two he was, or if he liked cities at all.

He scratched his head. 'Mr Acquah, please understand. In a couple of weeks I will be able to take a holiday, but in forensics you lose evidence every second. I can't afford to wait that long if I am to solve the case that they want me to work on. I'm only asking for an earlier holiday.' As he spoke, Kayo noticed how passive he had become. In a city rife with responsibility and thin on options, the flame of his usual defiance had dropped to a flicker.

Mr Acquah shook his head. 'Kayo, you are not listening to me. What is a small holiday, eh? My problem is with your Sergeant Whatever, who had the nerve to call you at my establishment . . .' His outrage seemed to rob him of words for an instant. '. . . without . . . without . . . without my permission.

There can be no progress on this matter unless the police have called to apologise.'

Kayo slammed the door as he left Mr Acquah's office, his chest full of air that he couldn't breathe out. The sea-blue walls of the corridor seemed to crash in on him. He barged past a surprised Joseph, shut the door to his office and picked up the waiting phone. 'Sergeant Mintah?'

'Yes, sah.'

'My boss says that your boss should call him.'

There was a silence. Sergeant Mintah chuckled. 'Your boss is a funny man.'

Kayo heard Sergeant Mintah's chair shift as it had earlier, then overheard him speaking to someone on the other side.

'His boss says Donkor should call him!'

There was loud laughter, then Sergeant Mintah's voice returned to the receiver. 'Tell your boss that this is a matter of national significance so it would not be in his best interests to intervene. I will expect your call, sah.'

The line went dead and Kayo replaced the receiver in its cradle. The phone rang again almost as soon as he put it down. It was probably Sergeant Mintah calling to leave his direct number, he thought. He grabbed his notepad, scribbled *National significance* and picked up the phone.

'Sergeant Mintah?'

'No, Kayo, it's Eunice. Sowah Scientific on the line for you.'

'Put them through.' Kayo exhaled and signalled for Joseph to come in.

*

Kayo pulled into Millie's Compound and parked beneath a neem tree to the left of the entrance. Millie's was in Cantonments, away from the chaos of Osu, on the side of the Danquah Circle where cars could actually move before 9 p.m.

Nii Nortey and his NGO cronies were already there, under the canopy of an umbrella close to the small building that housed the bar and storeroom. The rest of Millie's Compound was largely bare, with discrete islands of chairs clustered around Rothman's umbrellas in no particular order. Kayo's friends had positioned themselves at stumbling distance from the grill that kept the right wall of Millie's bar coal black. They were eating kebabs and laughing with drink-fuelled abandon. They were obviously on their second round of Star beer. Kayo exhaled his day and pulled his handbrake, feeling his tension dissipate slightly with the effort. He was looking forward to a cool drink.

As he opened the car door he heard a familiar chant and smiled. Nii Nortey and Sammy T had spotted him and begun the ritual known as 'chipping fans'. 'KO, KO.' They chanted his name at increasing volume until he raised his hands, acknowledged his fame and smiled. When he got to them, he traded the customary elaborate handshakes and endured the exaggerated compliments.

'Chale, e be you this? When you come fine so?'

'Chale, your shirt bright aah say I no dey fit look you!'

'I beg ooh, I beg,' Kayo pleaded, laughing as he sat in the chair Sammy T had pulled for him. He looked at the four men seated around him and shook his head. 'Chale, I'm laughing now but I had a terrible day at work.' He sighed and opened an extra button on his pale yellow shirt so the six o'clock breeze could reach his chest.

Akwasi, who was seated on Kayo's right next to Nii Nortey, raised his right arm and clicked his fingers. 'Waiter, please bring my man his usual Guinness.' He brought his arm down and tapped Kayo's chest.

Nii Nortey leaned forward to look past Akwasi. 'Oh, Kayo, before you start crying, I have to tell you: Auntie Millie has started serving roast chicken.'

All five men except Nii Nortey laughed.

'Ooh,' Nii Nortey protested. 'I'm serious. The thing is seriously good. I would insult my own mother just for a taste. Ask Dan.' He tapped the table closest to where the quietest of the group sat.

Dan was a risk analyst with the Rural Development Bank. He was okro-seed dark, with skin so smooth that it looked like patent leather and he always exposed his full set of teeth before he spoke. 'Nii Nortey, stop fooling. The man is in distress and all you can talk about is chicken.'

'Ooh, Dan, chale, just answer the question.' Nii Nortey stood up. 'Was the chicken good or not?'

Dan smiled. 'It was good.'

'Aha, so I'm going to order some more.' He walked off towards the bar.

Akwasi turned to Kayo. 'Don't mind Nortey; tell us what happened.'

The waiter arrived with Kayo's bottle of Guinness and poured it carefully into a narrow glass.

Kayo took a long draught, then looked up at Sammy T. 'Sammy, do you remember that I told you and Nortey I was going to try for the police job one last time?'

Sammy T nodded and motioned Nii Nortey to come and sit down.

'Well, I never got round to it. But today I was sitting in the lab when, out of the blue, I got a call from the police wanting me to help them with a case. Chale, I excite bassa bassa, but I kept cool. I told the man I had to ask my boss.'

'Oh, that fool Acquah?' Nii Nortey cut in. 'What did he say?'

'He said no.'

'Ah! You should leave,' Sammy T urged.

'Sammy, I can't just leave. You know how things are.'

'So what did the police say?' Akwasi asked.

'They told me to tell Acquah not to interfere, but he said no again. The second time he said if I ever bring up such nonsense again he will fire me.'

'Ooh, Kayo, that man can't fire you. You virtually run the place.' Nii Nortey slapped the table again.

'No, no, no, chale,' Dan said. 'You know how proud these private enterprise people are. He'll fire him just to brag to his girlfriend that he fired a UK graduate. Mark my words.'

'True ooh!' Akwasi chimed in.

Dan continued. 'Remember when I did the review on our loans and recommended that my boss freeze the credit of Makaho Cold Stores and seize Mr Osei's fleet of Jaguars? The man said he would demote me and give me a written warning because he had not asked me for any report. Ah! And we're talking about people who have never made a single payment on their loans. Not one! Makaho Stores has had a credit facility for four solid years.'

They all nodded as the waiter arrived with a whole roast chicken cut into chunks on a blue plate with shito on the side.

Kayo reached for one of the wings and sighed. 'Chale, I'm frustrated. You see how powerless we all are? Ah, I really felt like slapping Acquah's harmattan head.'

Nii Nortey took the chicken's tail and raised it to his lips. He looked at Kayo, said 'This is your boss's balls,' and started chewing.

Sammy T got up and slapped Nii Nortey's head. They all laughed, drowned their misgivings in drink, and chewed their chicken down to its fragile bones.

*

Kayo drove past Labone Secondary School towards the T-junction that led onto the Ring Road – *Accra's main artery*, his geography teacher used to say. Vendors sold their wares on both sides of Josiah Tongogara Street. The glow that their kerosene lamps cast on their faces gave them an ethereal look, but the spicy smell of their exertions, the pungent odour of the money they tied inside their waistcloths, kept them firmly rooted to earth. Kayo could distinguish the aromas of tsofi and fried yam, rice, kelewele and kenkey. The kenkey seller at Labone Junction was famous for the quality of her food and Kayo could see the steady mass of children sent to buy kenkey for their evening meals shrinking and growing like a lung. He considered stopping but he knew his mother would already have kenkey at home. Kayo glanced left, then turned right onto the road. Traffic near the junction was light for early evening but he knew there would be heavy traffic once he got closer to Kwame Nkrumah Circle. He could do a U-turn and head for the coast road, yet he carried on down Ring Road. On his right was a row of houses separated from the dual carriageway by a wide open gutter and a little-used street. The gutter had a series of wooden planks thrown across at intervals to serve as bridges to the main road where trotros would stop to pick up anyone who raised an arm and could pay the fare. At almost every one of these bridges was a trader, selling everything from loose change for taxi and trotro drivers, to chibom – fried egg sandwiches. Just past the row of houses was the US Embassy, painted white and walled off from the rest of Labone, identifiable from afar by its red, white and blue flag and assembly of satellite dishes. A convenient distance across the road from the embassy was a strip nicknamed Ashawo Lane, close to the former Black Caesar's Nightclub, where prostitutes paraded in outfits that seemed to have survived every major change in fashion for the last thirty years. As long as skirts were short, blouses were cut low, dresses were a size smaller than the ideal, and the colours were bright enough to catch an unsettled eye, they were in fashion. It was these pockets of life that made Kayo endure the traffic that Kwame Nkrumah Circle held in store for him. Even the quiet stretch between the main fire station building and Broadcasting House, where the new spaghetti interchange had been built, bristled with some intangible energy; taxi drivers honked their horns just so they could hear the echo as they streaked past the concrete erection.

Kayo had never learned to enjoy the streets of London in this way. He knew his East Street Market from Leadenhall, but he couldn't map them in his sleep like he could the twisted lanes, streets and heaving gutters between Osu's Night Market and Nima Market. For him London's streets were linked by the primary colours on the Underground map and abstract numbers marking bus routes. He saw little on bus rides, his eyes constantly scanning Bernard Knight's updated version of *Simpson's Forensic Medicine*, and often missed his stop, making his geography quite illogical. It would have been different if he drove, as he did in Birmingham later, but he couldn't afford a car while he was completing his medical studies at Imperial College, and by the time he started his specialisation in pathology at the Charing Cross Hospital, he was a dedicated user of public transport, very set in his ways. Kayo's specialisation was his first act of rebellion, the first time he realised that he was not inclined to follow the expected path if it didn't feel right. He had left home to study medicine and he did, but anaesthesiology, his original choice of specialisation, began to lose its lure the first time he opened a careers brochure at Imperial and saw the options open to him after his studies. Forensic pathology leaped out of the pages and he felt no fear of censure, no stirrings of doubt, as he decided to stay at Charing Cross for an extra two years, learning all he could about forensics. He never questioned why. It was only when he had to explain to his supervisor in forensic pathology why he absolutely wanted to pursue it that his grandfather's death came up.

The story came tumbling out, surprising him. He had found the old man face down on the beach, lifeless and cold. How could a man famed for rescuing his fellow fishermen, often far out at sea, drown in a couple of inches of water on the shore? He couldn't accept, as his grandfather's fellow fishermen had, that it was meant to be. His grandfather's life was not sunset, some light that went out whether you liked it or not. Nothing he had learned in all the lessons at school had prepared him for the possibility that Grandpa Okaikwei, who was still actively fishing at the age of fifty-nine, and had hard, ugly muscles like cocoyams, could die without being ill. The entire scenario reeked of foul play to him. Kayo had begun to regard some of the fishermen of Nyɛmashie with suspicion, but at the age of ten there wasn't much he could do. As time passed he'd let go of the targeted suspicions but the feeling of helplessness, the inability to make sense of his grandfather's death clung to him like a stench. In a way, his entire career was a search for answers.

Kayo never shared the story of his forensic pathology interview with anyone so it was difficult for him to explain to his friends why he was so attached to the idea of working as a forensics officer in Ghana; how so many deaths attributed to witchcraft and bad luck made his skin crawl with impatience, a longing to go in with his silver forensics case and present scientific answers, real answers.

He slowed his car down as he got to the traffic at Kwame Nkrumah Circle, shook his head at a beggar who approached him from the sidewalk, and rolled his window down. He thought about his friends and how their career choices reflected their character. Nii Nortey and Dan both worked as IT specialists for Danida. They were always on the move, troubleshooting, never getting too involved with anything because they dealt with too many people. If they didn't have the answers, they simply called someone who did. Kayo had come to realise that their approach to dealing with challenges in their personal lives was to drink; they rebooted in the morning and hoped things would be better. Dan was so cautious it was a surprise that he was the first of Kayo's friends to get married. In school he'd barely been able to ask for a dance, paralysed by thinking of all the possible outcomes of his request. But as a risk analyst he was perfect. In fact, Akwasi, who Kayo had only just met through Nii Nortey, turned out to be his most useful friend. A sociologist, he loved to talk things through, look into the wider implications of each action.

While the rest of the guys were laughing at Nii Nortey's jokes about working in Accra, Akwasi drew Kayo aside. The patient-doctor ratio in Ghana was something like 30,000 to 1, he said, so physicians were in high demand and it only took two years to get the four specialisations required to practise hospital medicine in Ghana. He asked Kayo why he didn't just quit working for Mr Acquah, do the specialisations training, and practise as a physician?

The question hovered over Kayo's observations as he emerged from the main stretch of congestion beyond Kwame Nkrumah Circle and drove past Awudome Cemetery towards Nyɛmashie.

Kayo parked his car under the mango tree to the left of his parents' compound and walked towards the square of light emerging from the mosquito netting on the top half of the outer door. He could tell by the smouldering coals on the coal pot to the left of the door that his mother had just finished cooking. A thin line of steam from the water she used to douse the fire still hung in the air like an unanchored umbilical cord. As he opened the door he heard his mother's voice from the dining room.

'My son the doctor, have you come?' His mother greeted him in Akuapem Twi, before switching to Ga so his father wouldn't feel left out. 'Okai, your son is home.' She raised her voice slightly so her husband would hear her over the drums that signalled that the seven o'clock news was about to begin on TV.

Kayo stooped to hug his mother and felt her rubbing his back as if he was still a boy.

'Kwadwo,' his father boomed, 'you are early today so you can eat with us.'

'Yes Father,' Kayo answered as he walked out of the dining room and continued left down a corridor towards the source of his father's voice. 'Let me go and change my clothes.' He undid the remaining buttons on his shirt and nodded in his father's direction when he reached the living-room door.

His father looked up from the news and smiled. His legs were stretched in front of him and his bare feet were propped up on a sheepskin cushion from Bolgatanga. He nodded back at Kayo and said, 'There is no greater joy for a man than to sit and eat with his son as a man,' and laughed, his square teeth glinting in the TV's light.

Kayo smiled, shook his head, and continued down the corridor. He wanted to stop and sit with his father, but he was tired and frustrated. He didn't want to burden his father with the knowledge that all was not well with him. It was better to smile and walk past, leaving his parents with the small joy they felt knowing their son was a 'doctor'.

He still hadn't been able to explain what his profession was. Things had been like that for a while. Ever since Kayo started boarding school there were parts of his life that he couldn't share. He understood them, but they didn't understand him. It was lonely, incredibly so. With his sister and brother both away from home, Kayo was now the only child in the house, and with that came extra attention. He sometimes got the feeling that his parents didn't feel fulfilled without their children.

The Odamtten home was divided down the middle by a corridor which ran from the front door to another door at the back leading to quarters in the rear where Kayo lived. The path from front to back door had been the dividing strip between his father's house and his grandfather's house. After his grandfather died, the two houses were gradually built into one as the family expanded. Growing up, Kayo loved to trace his fingers along the hidden lines where walls had been broken or built to join the two houses.

His room was unadorned, the right wall crammed with shelves and books, with a portable stereo on the central shelf. There was a sink at the end of the wall closest to the door, below which was a cane basket. Kayo threw his shirt into the basket and watched its pale yellow intensity disappear like daylight. He walked to his bed on the left side of the room, took off his shoes by stepping on the insoles, loosened his belt, wriggled out of his trousers and lay back on the bed with a sigh, his still-socked feet flat on the dark blue linoleum floor. The remote control for the stereo lay by his thigh and he reached for it. He pressed the power button and Kojo Antwi's voice seeped into the room. Within minutes Kayo was asleep.

He was startled awake by a series of heavy knocks on his door.
'Yes?'
'Kwadwo.' His father's voice had a hint of concern in it. 'Why, are you having a baby in there? Come and eat.'
'I'm coming, Father. I'm coming.'

benada

KAYO STARTED HIS CAR BEFORE HE NOTICED THE CRACK IN his windscreen. It ran from the top left edge of the glass halfway down, towards the base of his wipers, as though on a journey it never finished. He got out and walked around the car; there was no other visible sign of damage. It was obvious what had happened; with the mangoes on their tree in season, the dark green maze of the tree's leaves had become a beacon to all the children in Nyɛmashie. Since the Odamtten house was without walls, there was no stopping ardent boys from attacking the ripe orange fruits with missiles. A wayward stone must have landed on his car. Kayo shrugged and walked back to the driver's side. This was not a place where insurance would cover him, besides, it was a small blemish; the car was for driving, not for show. Having spent the night agonising over his missed opportunity with the police, he had finally decided that he was better off staying at Acquabio. If the police really wanted him, they would have to process his job application and offer him an actual job – not some random 'unclassified' case. Yes, he wanted to work as a forensic scientist, but not on a one-off case that would lead nowhere. He was more concerned about the systemic approach of the police; forensics should be a key part of law enforcement. Regardless, he found himself cringing at the thought of all the evidence ticking away at the scene of crime. He shrugged again as he eased into the car. As he did so, he spotted a ripe mango by his trailing left foot and bent to pick it up. He smiled; it wasn't such a bad day after all. The engine responded as soon as he turned the key and he reversed onto the dusty road beside their home that ran fifty metres towards the sea, where the Coast Road began.

Kayo liked to use the Coast Road in the morning; it made him feel connected to his family. His father went out to sea after Kayo went to bed and returned to land in the morning with the catch of the day. Kayo's mother and the other fish sellers waited on the shore for the fishermen to pull their nets in, then got to work separating the fish into species and sizes for sale. It was a familiar routine. During his school holidays he used to go out with his mother early in the morning and help his father's team of fishermen pull their nets in. He remembered the chants the men sang, the way the sun rose slow, as though it was tied to the ends of the nets they were pulling, then cast a brilliant peach glow across the surface as it gained shape. If you looked to the side you could see the light glance off the large aluminium basins that the fish sellers used; the pale glints flashed like winks from the horizon.

Kayo listened to the hum of his engine as he changed gears and sped down the coast. He had considered buying an in-car stereo but it wasn't a priority for him. His younger brother, Kakra, would soon finish his National Service assignment and start university; that meant he would be paying accommodation costs for both his siblings. Thankfully his sister only had another year of study to complete. He pulled into the Acquabio car park, reached across to the glove compartment for his mobile phone, and alighted.

Joseph was the only technician in at 7:30 a.m. and as Kayo said good morning to him he made a mental note to recommend him for a pay rise. In fact he would ask for a pay rise himself; he had had enough of being taken for granted.

There was a stack of laboratory result sheets in the tray he kept on top of the grey filing cabinet. Kayo grabbed them and flicked through as he settled into his chair. He was relieved to find they were all for straightforward ingredient and product tests; there were no medical results, and this meant a lighter day. Whenever there were medical samples to analyse, Kayo liked to go into the lab and repeat all the tests himself before making any diagnoses. It was his way of reminding himself that he was dealing with human lives, that his work was still important. Results from ingredient and product tests simply required him to write basic reports outlining whether or not the samples supplied met the required government standards, and, if not, why.

When Kayo joined Acquabio, he'd added a recommendations section to the reports to advise firms on what changes they could make to their processes to improve their chances of meeting the Ghana Standards Board grade, or to raise levels of consistency and quality. He later found out in conversation with a client that Mr Acquah had slapped a five per cent premium onto the cost of the reports immediately after Kayo started doing the recommendations. He was an astute businessman – Kayo couldn't begrudge him that.

At 8:00 a.m. the radio kicked in. Kayo looked up to see the lab suddenly full. His seven technicians were evenly spaced around the central lab benches. The two women in the team were talking across the benches while setting up their clamps and Bunsen burners, and Joseph was standing by the radio, lowering the volume. Hugh Masekela's 'Zulu Wedding' was playing; it was a song Kayo liked, but he resisted the urge to signal Joseph to turn it up. From his window view he quietly savoured the sanitised order of the lab; perfectly parallel benches with white Formica surfaces, elongated wood stools with square seats, a row of micro-centrifuges, spare burette clamps, test-tube racks and reagents on the side bench, above which Kayo had stuck posters with laboratory safety instructions after he impressed the importance of health and safety procedures upon Mr Acquah.

Kayo returned to the results Joseph had delivered. They consisted of graphs with comments and bullet-point summaries noting the tests each sample had been subjected to and whether it passed or failed. Kayo picked up the floppy disk Joseph had left by his computer and slotted it in the drive. It had a copy of Joseph's summaries in a Word document, from which Kayo copied and pasted excerpts into his reports. He kept the file open while he worked on each report and transferred the relevant section when he got to it. When a report was finished, he printed it out for Joseph to take to Eunice to have it bound. Joseph then brought the bound report back to him to sign.

Kayo got into a steady rhythm working on the reports and was shocked when Joseph knocked on his door to say he was leaving for the day. It was 5:15 p.m. already. Kayo gathered the printed and bound reports that Joseph had placed on his desk and signed them with a flourish. He felt quite accomplished; in addition to preparing all the reports, he had reviewed his budget and felt he could make a strong case to Mr Acquah to increase his department's allocation. Now working hours were officially over, he slipped Stevie Wonder's *Innervisions* CD into his computer and began to tidy his desk. He clicked his fingers to 'Too High' as he placed the signed reports on the left of the desk for Joseph to pick up in the morning, and put his pad, with all his random scribbling, in his top drawer. On the computer, Kayo saved his budget spreadsheet and closed his

Excel window. He was closing the Word template he had developed for his reports when the phone rang.

'Hello?'

'Odamtten.'

It sounded like the sergeant from the day before. Kayo frowned and glanced at his watch. 'Sergeant Mintah?'

'Correct first time, sah. I can tell you will be a good man to work with.'

'I told you yesterday that my boss wouldn't allow me to take time out to help you.'

'He hasn't changed his mind?' The sergeant's voice rose slightly.

'No.'

There was silence, then a chuckle at the other end. 'No problem. So, have you given thought to leaving the job, sah?'

'Actually, I have,' said Kayo, pulling his pad back out of his drawer and doodling *NO* on the pale cream lined paper, 'and I've decided not to leave. I need the money.'

Sergeant Mintah released a long, healthy laugh. 'We all need money, sah, we all need money.' He paused, then chuckled. 'I'll speak to you tomorrow then.'

'I won't change my mind.' Kayo's pad was now covered with *NO*s in a forest of black squiggles.

'I know, but it is my job to get you to work with us, so I will call you.' The sergeant paused. 'You are an interesting man, Odamtten, an interesting man.'

The line went dead and Kayo noticed the office was turning dark. He put his pad back in the top drawer and stared at the screen until the screensaver came on. Swirls of green, blue, red and yellow played on his face as he sat there, his mind blank as Stevie sang 'Don't You Worry 'Bout A Thing'. Later he would think of this moment and be amazed that he had been unaware of Stevie Wonder's voice during his conversation with Sergeant Mintah.

When Kayo looked at his watch again it was 6:48 p.m. He switched on his mobile phone and immediately heard a beep. It was a text message from Nii Nortey: *bloody fool! the man no dey respect u wey u dey tear overtime. hurry up then come millie's make we drink. kwasia.* Kayo laughed out loud; Nii Nortey found it impossible to send a text message without beginning and ending it with insults. Kayo pressed the green button on his Nokia twice and waited for the distant dial.

Nii Nortey picked up where his text left off. 'Stupid man. How can you make your friends wait for you this long? You better report for drinking duties immediately.'

'Kwasia yourself, what did you mean by that text message? How do you know I wasn't somewhere with your girlfriend?'

'Because I know your useless arse. You dey love work! As for my girlfriend, I dey bed inside plus am the whole day wey I no see you for there.'

Kayo held his phone away from his ear so he wouldn't be deafened by Nii Nortey's hysterical laugh, then brought it back when the laughter died down. 'OK, Nortey, I dey come, but I no go fit dey there more than one hour; I tire.'

'You come. We'll talk about how long you stay later.'

'OK. Oh, chale, please make sure there's a Guinness waiting for me.'

'No problem.'

*

The spot of light splintered through the crack in his windscreen, partially blinding him. Kayo slowed down as the car in front of him manoeuvred round the barrier the police had set up near the main fire station on Ring Road. When he reached the grille, a tall policeman with two tribal marks on his left cheek flashed a torch quickly over his number plate, then brought the light to rest on his face.

41

Kayo squinted.

The policeman nodded at his companion, a man almost as tall as him but twice his width, 'Sergeant Ofosu, I think this is our man.'

Sergeant Ofosu, who was chewing on groundnuts, smiled, showing clumps of half-chewed kernels around his teeth as he did so.

The first policeman looked at Kayo and said, 'Ei, this man, you want to make us work.'

Kayo leaned out of his window. 'Can I ask why I've been stopped please?'

Sergeant Ofosu started laughing. 'Can you ask what?' He patted his chest. 'I am the law. You have been stopped for whatever reason I choose.' He turned to his companion. 'Garba, radio the other units and tell them to remove all the roadblocks in the city. This is definitely our man; a been-to in a second-hand VW Golf who asks big questions.' He touched the side of Kayo's door with his baton. 'My friend, park and get out. We have been waiting for you.'

'Sergeant, you still haven't told me why I've been stopped.'

Sergeant Ofosu rapped hard on Kayo's door. 'My friend, do you want me to break your legs or something? I said get out. If you want things to be simple you'll just do as I say.'

Kayo eased his car onto the side of the dual carriageway and parked. He opened his door partially and squeezed out of the car. He looked at the part of the door that had been struck with the baton to see if the paintwork had suffered and turned to face Sergeant Ofosu who was walking towards him. 'OK, I'm out now.'

The sergeant smiled. 'Constable Garba, come and take notes,' he shouted.

Garba hoisted the roadblocks to the side of the road and ran to join the sergeant, rubbing his hands clean as he moved.

When he was in position he took a notebook from his top pocket and Sergeant Ofosu spoke.

'So, my friend, what is your full name and occupation?'

'Kayo Odamtten. I'm a scientist.'

'Is that the name your father outdoored you with?' Sergeant Ofosu's voice was a mix of impatience, amusement and cynicism. 'Give me your real name.'

'Kwadwo Okai Odamtten.'

Sergeant Ofosu nodded. 'That's it? No English names?'

'No.'

'Garba.' Sergeant Ofosu turned to the other officer. 'I think he's one of your people. No Christian name.'

'Sergeant, I beg to differ—' Garba started.

'Garba, this is no time to beg. We are interrogating a suspect.'

Kayo took a quick glance at the cars passing by. It was still early evening. He was worried that someone he knew might pass by. Someone might tell his family he had been arrested and they would worry unnecessarily. In many ways Accra was a small city. He cleared his throat. 'Sergeant, you still haven't told me why I have been stopped.'

'So, where is this Kayo from?'

'What?'

'I said, this Kayo name, which your father didn't give you, where is it from?'

'It's from university. I studied in London and nobody could say my name properly, so I made it up.'

'Aha, university man. No wonder you are asking me big questions.' He turned to Garba. 'Are you writing all this?'

'Yes, Sergeant.'

'So, my friend Kayo, what kind of scientist are you?'

'I'm a trained physician.'

'A doctor?' Sergeant Ofosu frowned for the first time that

43

evening. His pale brown forehead bunched like unironed linen. 'Are you sure?'

'Yes.'

Sergeant Ofosu tilted his head to study Kayo's face. He tapped his baton twice against his side, then put it back in his wide black belt. He reached into his trouser pocket for a handful of groundnuts, tossed them in his mouth and started chewing. 'So, my friend, are you just a doctor, or are you hiding something?' he asked

'I'm hiding nothing. I'm a physician, but I specialised in forensics. I don't practise hospital medicine.'

Sergeant Ofosu smiled. 'Garba.' He tapped his colleague on the shoulder. 'We have our man.'

Garba slipped his notebook back into his pocket and reached for his handcuffs. He looked sad as he reached for Kayo's left arm. 'Kwadwo Okai Odamtten, I am placing you under arrest for attempts to destabilise the government.'

Kayo released a high-pitched gasp and opened his mouth. Instinctively, he shrugged Garba's hand off. 'What?' He swung his gaze from Garba to Sergeant Ofosu like a metronome. 'Are you joking?'

Sergeant Ofosu shook his head like a disappointed parent. 'My friend,' he tapped the pistol on his right hip, 'I'm sure you know the harsh consequences of resisting arrest. We are just doing our job.' His eyes held Kayo's, then he turned to Garba. 'No need for handcuffs, Constable.'

Garba nodded.

Kayo managed one last protest. 'How am I supposed to be destabilising the government?'

Sergeant Ofosu looked at him. 'I know you are a Muslim like my friend Garba here, but I'm sure you've heard that line from the Bible, "He that is not with me is against me."' He gestured towards a dark blue Range Rover parked ten metres up the road. The white crest of the Ghana Police glowed on its side. 'Come with me.'

Kayo shook his head with his hands turned up, as though begging for alms. His frustration made the left side of his head palpitate. 'I am not Muslim,' he said to the sergeant's back. The man moved surprisingly fast for someone his size. His black uniform blended with the dark so Kayo could mainly see the flash of his wristwatch as he swung his arms.

'Garba, lock his car and radio the boys to come for it.'

Inside the vehicle, the sergeant sat beside Kayo in the back seat and turned to face him.

'So, where did you go today?'

'What do you mean?'

'Yesterday, you were at home by 7 p.m., it is now 8:15 p.m.'

Kayo decided not to ask the obvious question. He loosened his patterned blue tie and rolled up the sleeves of his shirt. 'I had a long day at work, then I went to meet some friends for a quick drink.'

'Ah, we all have long days, my friend. Today is yours, tomorrow might be mine.' He laughed, releasing a waft of crushed groundnuts, reminding Kayo that he had not eaten.

'Will I be given food?'

Garba appeared, opened the front door and sat in the driver's seat. 'Everything is settled, Sergeant.'

'Good. Garba, do a U-turn and take us to Blue Gate Chop Bar. I am going to feed our special prisoner before we lock him up.' He turned to Kayo like an old friend, addressing him by his first name this time. A name only his family used. 'Kwadwo, I hope you like banku. You will have to eat in the car with us, like a policeman.'

Kayo's cell was a disused office in the Police Headquarters building. The windows had been reinforced with the kind of iron rods used on building sites. They hadn't even been treated for rust. It was obviously just routine. It would be stupid to try to escape from the building.

'This is our special cell. For high-level prisoners.' Sergeant Ofosu said it with a hint of pride. There was a worn red leather sofa against the wall to the right of the door and a water cooler in one corner. The floor was terrazzo and bare. A kerosene lamp that Garba had brought with him from the main entrance illuminated the room. There was no source of electricity.

'I see,' said Kayo.

Sergeant Ofosu reached for the lamp and turned to leave. 'Sleep well, my friend. We shall meet again in the morning.' The yellow light of the lamp shrank as the door shut with a firm snap.

Night swallowed the space and Kayo heard three sets of bolts fall into place in quick succession. He felt for the edge of the sofa, lay back and closed his eyes. His head was still throbbing. He was mad at himself for not thinking of the right things to say. He hadn't even asked to see a warrant. He smiled, feeling a hint of weariness pulling the edges of his mouth down. It probably wouldn't have made a difference. He would be more assertive in the morning. He remembered they hadn't searched him and reached into his pocket for his mobile phone. His frantic fumbling yielded nothing. he had left it in his glove compartment. Typical. He emptied his pockets onto the floor and entertained himself by guessing the contents by touch. It wasn't difficult. A handkerchief, penknife, two capsules of PK chewing gum, and his wallet. Not much. He felt a stroke of breeze from his left and opened his eyes. There was an open window on the wall at about chest level. It had no mosquito netting or refinements and looked out over Labone, towards the sea. It was a clear night and the stars were in full attendance. The lights from the residential area were cheap baubles by comparison. The window was too small for anyone to fit through, but he wasn't worried about that. In a few minutes the mosquitoes would sense his body heat and he would be food for all comers. He returned to the couch, rolled his sleeves back down to his wrists, and reclined. Resigned to his fate.

wukuda

KAYO WOKE UP AN HOUR BEFORE HE HEARD THE BOLTS ON THE
door being released. He did some push-ups, sit-ups and five
minutes standing on his head, to get his mind and body sharp.
He was primed for battle. Kayo could think of no reason why
he should be arrested, unless it was connected with the phone
calls he had received in the last two days. He had not memor-
ised the names of the officers involved, but perhaps they were
mixed up in a plot and he had been arrested because they had
contacted him. Maybe there was another reason; maybe something to do with Nii Nortey and his drinking friends. Kayo
quickly shook the idea out of his head; Nii Nortey wouldn't
know how to hijack a fruit stall. Either way, this was no way
to arrest a suspect. It was not the proper way to work. If he
ever did work for the police, would this be the kind of protocol
within which he would have to work? Kayo stood and swung
his arms in a circle, then bent down to touch his toes. He was
going to demand his legal rights and get released. This was
harassment.

The door creaked to reveal Garba in a crisp starched
uniform. Free of the sweat of a day's policing, he looked
youthful, about the same age as Kayo, maybe slightly younger
– mid-twenties. Even Sergeant Ofosu looked different in
daylight. Kayo noticed that he hadn't yet worn his cap. His
hair was a neat helmet and he had a ready smile.

'Ah, my friend, you are up. You didn't sleep well?'

'I did. Just a few mosquito bites.'

Sergeant Ofosu patted Kayo's back. 'Good man.' He held out a small package. 'I brought you a meat pie. They will not feed you in interrogation.'

Kayo took it with his right hand and transferred it to his left. 'I am not going to interrogation. I want to make some phone calls.'

Sergeant Ofosu exchanged a look with Garba. Kayo noticed and decided to push their uncertainty to his advantage. He tried once more to remember the name of the officer who had asked for him to be contacted, but he couldn't.

'My friend, we have instructions to take you to interrogation.'

Kayo walked to the open window on the left and looked out. The blue sky offered no answers. On the coast palm trees swayed like waving hula dancers, taunting him. He raised the package in his left hand and unwrapped it. It looked good. He smelled it and took a bite. An airy pocket of warm chicken, chilli, tomato and flour suffused his mouth. He closed his eyes.

'Is it good?' Sergeant Ofosu was watching him.

'It's very good. Where did you buy it?'

'My wife makes them.' Sergeant Ofosu smiled and placed his cap lightly on his head. 'Shall we go?'

'No.' Kayo took another bite of the pie. 'I would like to speak to the PCC; I can't remember his name.' If he had been arrested because of his links to the officer, he wanted to meet the man, at least.

A wave of puzzlement washed over Sergeant Ofosu's face. He looked towards the door, where Garba was standing almost to attention.

'PRCC,' offered Garba, 'Donkor.'

'Yes,' Kayo clicked his fingers. 'Yes, I would like to speak to Inspector P. J. Donkor.'

Sergeant Ofosu fixed Garba with a stern look, then barked: 'Garba, how many times do I have to tell you? Call your superiors by their name and title.'

'Sorry, Sergeant. Inspector Donkor, Sergeant.'

Kayo strode to the middle of the room. 'I would like to speak to Inspector P. J. Donkor, please.'

'Garba, go and find out if he's here.' Sergeant Ofosu sat on the edge of the old sofa. 'Now, my friend, I can't make any promises, but we will try for you.'

'Thank you.'

'The pie was good?'

Kayo nodded.

'She wants to start catering. You think she'll do well?'

Kayo nodded again.

'The view is not bad, eh?' Sergeant Ofosu rubbed his hands and pointed at the building next door. 'CID; I wanted to work there, paa. Investigations. But because I schooled in the village I had no connections. CID is full of you city boys; they put the rest of us on the road.' He sighed. 'But it's not too bad. Ah, where's Garba?' He tapped the side of the sofa and stood up. 'In fact let's go downstairs. The inspector's office is on the second floor.'

The inspector was a short dark man with greying hair at his temples. He had an intense stare and a twitch in his left cheek. There was a plaque in black and gold with his full name *Percival Joseph Donkor* and, beneath it, his title – *Police Regional Coordinating Chief.* He dismissed Garba and Sergeant Ofosu with a tired wave of his hands and indicated a chair for Kayo to sit in. He formed a pyramid with his hands and rested his twitch against it, as though he was preparing to sleep.

He moved to adjust the paperweight on his right so that it

was at a forty-five-degree angle to the edge of the desk. He leaned his cheek back against his pyramid.

'So, you are Kayo Odamtten.'

'Yes.'

'You are young.' He made it sound like an accusation.

'Yes.'

'I hear you want to make phone calls.'

'Yes. But I wanted to speak to you as well. I think you may be the reason I was arrested.'

'Have you watched *Law & Order*?' The man didn't seem to have heard him.

'Yes.'

The inspector laughed, exposing the tiniest teeth Kayo had ever seen. They looked like they belonged to a mouse or a puppy. This was no friend or co-accused; he was the brains behind Kayo's arrest.

'So you want two phone calls?'

'Yes, three if possible.'

The inspector pushed his black telephone across the table towards Kayo. Everything in the office was black, except the floor, the edges of the table and cabinets, and the window frames, which were wood. Wawa, deep brown, from the Ashanti region. It was a good thing the windows were large, otherwise the office would have felt like the inside of a coffin.

Kayo picked up the handset to dial, but the inspector held up his hand.

'Before you call, you are aware that you have been arrested for plotting the overthrow of the government, right?'

'For attempting to destabilise the government, they said.'

'Well, it is now more serious. We have arrested two of your co-conspirators who have confessed that you were planning a deal to import light firearms into the country yesterday

51

between 1000 hours and 1200 hours. Can you account for your whereabouts?'

'Of course. I was at work.'

'Well, I would make that your first priority. Otherwise I will have no choice but to move you to a maximum security establishment.'

Kayo exhaled. He was beginning to smell his own stench. He hadn't showered since yesterday and he was sweating. 'Can I call my workplace?'

The inspector opened his arms.

'Good morning, Acquabio Research, can I help you?'

'Good morning Eunice, can you put me through to Mr Acquah?'

'Hold the line, please.'

Kayo frowned. Eunice usually had more to say to him than 'Hold the line'. He looked up at the inspector. He was smiling. There was a shuffle and a cough on the other end.

'Yes, good morning, who is this?'

'Mr Acquah, it's me, Kayo.'

'Kayo who? I don't know anyone by that name.'

'Kayo Odamtten. Your senior researcher. Don't you recognise my voice?' Kayo moved the handset to his left hand. His palms had less traction than silk.

'Look, young man, I don't know who you are talking about. This is a busy laboratory and I don't have much time.'

'But, Mr Acquah—'

There was a click. Then silence. Kayo looked up at Inspector Donkor. He was smiling again. Kayo wanted to crush his mouse jaw.

'OK, so what's going on here? I would like to play your games, but I don't have time. If I am here for conspiracy why am I not at CID next door?'

'Mr Kayo, please remember who you are talking to.'

The inspector's voice was as even as the objects arranged on his desk. His left cheek twitched once. 'You said you wanted three phone calls. That was one. Do you want the other two?'

'No, Inspector, I don't mean to be rude, but I want to know what's going on.'

Inspector Donkor sat back in his armchair. Kayo observed for the first time that the top of the man's head was level with the back of the black leather chair.

'Do you know how this country is run?'

'No.' Kayo meant it.

'Well, the police force is Civil Service, so is the prison service, the fire service, ports and harbours and the military. I'm sure you know that.'

Kayo nodded.

'The thing is the higher levels of the Civil Service are not attained by merit, or number of years of service. It's purely by appointment. That means the ministers decide who becomes the chief of police – IGP.' Inspector Donkor pulled open a drawer and removed a large laminated sheet. He placed it on the table and spread it out. It was an organisational chart. 'I am an ambitious man. This post,' he pointed at his plaque, 'did not even exist until I was given it. I am now three levels below the highest post in the police force.' He stabbed his finger at the chart. 'I intend to get to the top before I retire. Are you with me?'

'I think I understand.'

The inspector replaced the chart and closed the drawer carefully. 'Now, my man Sergeant Mintah called you on Monday about a job. I understand you wanted to do it but your boss, Mr Acquah, would not give you time off.'

'That's true.'

'I also understand that some years ago, you applied to join the force and were turned down.' His mouth had the beginnings of a smile that Kayo wanted to stamp on.

'Yes, eleven months ago.'

'Then we understand each other.'

'No, Inspector, I still don't understand.' Kayo clenched his fist beneath the table. The man spoke in concentric circles. The words came from the same place but drew entirely individual paths.

Inspector Donkor smiled. 'Have you watched *CSI*?'

'Yes.'

'That's you.' He gave Kayo a meaningful look.

Kayo frowned. Still confused.

'I hear you are a forensics man.'

'I am.'

'So, we have a case in a village near Tafo that we need your help with. It is not even a case we would have bothered with, but the minister for roads and highways is sleeping with a girl from Tafo. She discovered some human matter and the minister himself called me that day to ask me to deploy some men. Now he is interested in the results.' The inspector tapped the edge of his table with his middle finger as if he was counting seconds. 'The minister's interest means opportunity for promotion. Not just promotion, but also bonuses. Bonuses are the lifeblood of the Civil Service. Our official salaries are a joke.' He laughed heartily.

Kayo was surprised at how melodious the laugh sounded. He smiled.

The inspector rebuilt his pyramid. 'And for you, maybe, if you are successful, a new job. Head of new forensics techniques.'

'And what if I am not successful?'

'Shall we not talk about failure? It makes me uncomfortable.' The inspector's cheek twitched twice.

Now that Kayo knew the inspector needed him, he had to look after himself. He rubbed his hands on his trousers and looked at the patterns on the wood floor. It wasn't a classic parquet pattern. It was individual diamonds with one dark diamond in the middle of each cluster of eight light ones. Kayo tapped his foot lightly on the floor. It was quality wood. He sat up and made his own pyramid. 'Have I lost my job at Acquabio?'

'I'm afraid so.'

'Then I need a guarantee of payment equivalent to six months' salary before I do the job.'

The inspector grinned. Showing his full rack of tiny teeth. 'A fighting man. I like that. Deal. Anything else?'

'I want it regardless of the outcome.'

Inspector Donkor's cheek twitched. 'OK. But you have to prepare a full *CSI*-style report for me to give to the minister.'

'Fine. Tell me about the case.'

'No time.' The inspector reached to the left of his desk and passed a folder to Kayo. 'Read it on your way there. Garba will be your driver. Good luck.' He stretched his body across the desk to shake Kayo's hand. His grasp was rough and vice-like. 'Garba!'

Kayo stood and heard the call relayed in the corridor before the tall constable appeared.

Garba stood to attention beside Kayo while Inspector Donkor barked orders.

Kayo barely listened. He put the folder that the inspector had given him under his left arm and gazed out of the window behind the inspector. It was the same view he had had from his overnight cell, except that, because he was now on a lower floor, he couldn't see as far as the waving palm trees. Kayo was certain that he would have to take his personal forensics case from home because he doubted that the Ghana Police would have what he needed. He wondered what to tell his parents about last night, then remembered that since he was detained on a Tuesday his father would have gone to sea after midnight, and his mother would have slept early in order to go to trade in the morning. As long as he got his car back to the house it would be fine.

Garba was impassive as Kayo followed him out of the building. Kayo waited for him at the main entrance while he brought a weathered dark blue Land Rover Defender to pick him up.

The constable parked, jumped down and opened the passenger door for Kayo. 'Yes sah.'

Kayo frowned and eased himself into the seat.

'Where to, sah?' Garba asked once he was at the wheel.

'Where is my car?' Kayo splayed his fingers on the dashboard as it dawned on him that Garba was now taking orders from him.

'In the rear yard, sah.'

'The keys?'

Garba reached into his top pocket and took out the familiar keys.

'OK. Take me to the car and follow me home.'

'Sah,' Garba hesitated for a moment. His right hand hovered over the gear stick. 'My orders are that you should be in Tafo within three hours.'

Kayo turned to face him. 'Garba, listen to me. If we don't go to my house, arriving in three hours will be useless. I know you have your orders but none of you understand what I have to do, otherwise I wouldn't be here. Are we clear?'

Garba shifted the Land Rover into gear and swung the car round in silence.

Kayo had finished reading the documents in the inspector's folder by the time Garba had driven past the University of Ghana at Legon and reached the outskirts of the Greater

Accra region. He placed the brown folder on the Land Rover's dashboard and studied the vegetation whipping by. The flora was just beginning to change from savannah to a thicker, greener variety and Kayo felt a freshness in the breeze. He tried to adjust his seat back but it wouldn't budge. From the corner of his eye he caught Garba looking at him with the beginnings of a smile. It was the first sign of life the constable had shown since Kayo had made him trail his VW Golf home so Kayo could park the car and pick up his case. Kayo ignored Garba's sullen demeanour and concentrated on the documents the inspector had given him. The account given by the person who had discovered the alleged remains, whose name had been blacked out in the files, was barely coherent; it was only remarkable for the repetitive use of the word *evil*. The police investigating unit's report was more structured and had a list of persons who had been interviewed, with several notes relating to an elderly man called Opanyin Poku. Kayo mentally crossed *theft, smuggling, trafficking* and *fraud* off his initial list of possible crimes, leaving *abduction* and *murder*. The signed document from the pathologist called to the scene didn't confirm that the remains were human but he had to assume they were. Kayo slouched in the seat and sighed.

Garba reached under Kayo's seat with his right hand and the back moved with a sudden, violent shudder.

Kayo cast a sharp look at Garba and then tried to adjust the seat again. This time it moved. Kayo leaned back and closed his eyes. The damp smell of the forest and the sound of the engine's turbodiesel hum intensified. Kayo tried to distinguish the smells of different plants, although he didn't know what they were. He pondered the challenges ahead, hoping the crime scene had not been unduly tampered with. It felt odd being driven to an assignment, having the time to mull over details and formulate a plan of action. When he worked for West Midlands Police, he drove, often alone, to every crime scene. Since he was on call almost the entire year he lived in Birmingham, he never took his equipment out of his Vauxhall Astra. There was no time to take in the routes he travelled; an address was shouted down a crackling radio, and he was off, mapping his way across a city he would never know. A city of corpses and statistical targets.

'Your boss likes prostitutes.'

Kayo opened his eyes slowly and looked at Garba. 'What?'

'Your boss. Did you know he frequented brothels?'

'Mr Acquah?'

'Yes. You didn't know?'

'No.' Kayo shrugged. 'Is that how your inspector scared him?'

'Ei, don't mention Donkor in such conversations.' Garba wiped his forehead with a red handkerchief. 'All the operational work for your case was done by Mintah.'

'I see.'

'Your man is a coward, eh. Mintah caught him in Osu picking up a girl.'

'But it's not a crime to pick up a girl, is it?'

'Sah, she was very young . . . about fifteen, sixteen, and Mintah had seen him taking her to a notorious hotel the night before.'

'So, have you charged him? Is he going to court?'

'Oh, sah, you know how things work. We have other things on him; he confessed to evading taxes and duping his business partner – one Belgian woman. Your man was afraid paa. He talked like a baby goat.'

'So why is he still free?'

'Sah—'

'Please call me Kayo.'

Garba nodded and carried on. 'He is more useful to us on

the outside. He runs a business; we can't just close it down. People need work.'

'I see.' Kayo closed his eyes again, his mind a multitude of grey spaces. As much as he sought justice, he understood the system. An average jury wouldn't take a prostitute seriously; it would be a waste of public money and would probably destroy whatever chance the girl still had to switch to a more conventional life. Men like Mr Acquah sometimes fell in love with these girls and kept them as mistresses, or, in some cases, married them. In an odd way the police were guided by an inclination to keep the peace, the way elders in the villages had done for centuries. But, he felt, they were also guided by greed; a free Mr Acquah would pay his tax arrears, but he would also be forever grateful to Sergeant Mintah for not putting him in jail. He would express that gratitude in regular gifts, cash gifts at Christmas and Easter, and other favours when needed.

'Mr Kayo, we are almost there.'

They were on a recently tarred road, maintained to the highest standard, in contrast to most of the other roads he had travelled on that far inland. Trees hung low over the road like a canopy, leaving a narrow strip of sunshine in the middle. He could make out some oil palm and stinging nettles in between the larger trees, but he couldn't tell what the larger trees were, except for the odd acacia dotted here and there. They were in rich, vertiginous forest. The density was only occasionally broken up by bright red, yellow and white flowers, and the pendulous fruits that hung from the trees.

Garba tapped Kayo on the left shoulder and pointed at a huge tree with clusters of dark green leaves. 'Do you know the name of that tree?'

'No.'

Garba chuckled. 'Bediwunua. It seems if your own sister wears the perfume from it you will want to fuck her.'

Kayo didn't respond. He felt as if Garba was trying to test him, find out what his limits were.

'What makes you think you can solve this case, kraa?'

Kayo shook his head. 'I never said I would solve it. I said I would investigate it; the two are very different.'

'It's a waste of time. Ofosu said the people are uncooperative and have no respect for the police. You can't proceed with inquiries. Can you even speak Twi?'

'Oh, I see your problem. You think because I studied abroad I have forgotten what it is to be Ghanaian.'

'No, Mr Kayo, it's just my concern. A whole unit of nine men couldn't find anything, and then they bring Mr One-Man-Thousand.'

Kayo laughed out loud. 'Garba, why do you think you are here? You are part of my team. This is not how I wanted to work for the police, but we have a job to do and I need your help. I'm not Mr One-Man-Thousand.'

Garba fell silent and turned onto a worn track by the side of the tarred road.

They came to a clearing where an old man sat holding a radio to his right ear. He was very dark-skinned, with a shaved head and, although he bore the wiry muscles of a long-distance runner, Kayo put his age at about sixty-five years old. The man was in the shadow of a large tree behind which spread a small village dotted with trees. Kayo recognised some fan palms and neem trees; the log the old man was sitting on was a felled palm. As Garba pulled the Land Rover to a stop, the old man stood and peered inside the car. Within seconds a trickle of kids had surrounded the car and were singing. A tall, lithe policeman with a complexion reminiscent of dried corn husks emerged from a cluster of huts to the right of the village, with a semi-automatic rifle slung casually in front of him. His eyes were red and puffed.

He walked up to Kayo and Garba, gave a mock salute and shook Garba's hand. 'Garba, you have brought the graduate?'

Garba nodded and turned towards Kayo. 'Mr Kayo, this is Mensah. He's a detective constable.' He turned back to his colleague. 'Where is the scene?'

Mensah gestured in the direction he came from and started walking.

Kayo tapped Garba's arm, signalling for him to wait. He walked up to the old man and greeted him in Akuapem Twi.

'Egya, I greet you.'

The old man smiled. He had a full set of strong-looking teeth and there was a chewing stick at the corner of his mouth.

'I respond.' He took hold of the hand Kayo had extended.

'Excuse me, my name is Kayo and I have come to do some work with the police. Could you take me to the chief to ask for permission?'

'What did you say they call you?'

'I'm called Kayo.'

'Is that your actual name?'

'No, Egya, it is Kwadwo Okai Odamtten.'

'Then I'll call you Kwadwo. I'm called Opanyin Poku.' The old man nodded, still gripping Kayo's hand. 'Where is your mother from?'

'She was born in Accra, but her father was from Kibi.'

The old man nodded, and then led Kayo away.

Garba followed them.

The hut that DC Mensah eventually led Kayo and Garba to was cordoned off with stakes fashioned from the branches of nearby trees and bushes, and strips of pale fabric. To the far left of the cordoned area was a dark blue tent with a camping stove in front of it.

As they approached the entrance of the hut, Kayo stopped and balanced his forensics kit on his thigh. He took out three pairs of gloves and a set of small numbered tags. He handed one pair of gloves each to DC Mensah and Constable Garba, who pulled them on with a look of intense unwillingness. Or was it distaste? Kayo wasn't sure. He wore the last pair himself and snapped his case shut. There was a heap of charcoal to the left of the hut's front, and what appeared to be debris from a broken pot. Kayo could smell the stench that had been highlighted in the police report; it reminded him of the foul remnants of a rat he had once found in the basement of his ground-floor flat in Birmingham.

Garba frowned and held his nose.

Kayo squatted by the debris and put a tag beside the charcoal heap. 'Garba, can you see how many pieces of this pot you can find?'

'Yes sah.'

'Please don't move them; just find them.' Kayo spotted a shining black stone beneath the hang of the doorway screen mat and looked up. 'Mensah, what is that?'

'That one is Bosomtwe stone.'

'From the lake?'

'Yes, from the crater. They used to put it in the pots to cool the water. The breakages by the hut are from his water cooler.'

Kayo noticed that Mensah dropped his 'h's when he spoke, but he sounded knowledgeable. Kayo had learned from Opanyin Poku that a cocoa farmer called Kofi Atta had lived alone in the hut, so Kayo anticipated that it shouldn't be difficult to dust for fingerprints. 'Garba, how many pieces did you find?'

'Seventeen.'

'Please label them.' Kayo passed Garba tags numbered two to eighteen.

'What for, sah? We know the cooler was broken; it's already in the report. We have to hurry. It stinks like the Korle over here.'

Kayo smiled at the casual reference to the Korle lagoon, which ran so close to where he lived in Nyɛmashie.

'Garba, I work differently. I need a lot more detail. I'll explain everything after we process the scene.' Kayo turned to the other policeman. 'Mensah, do you know how to dust for finger-prints?'

'For sure.' Mensah nodded with enthusiasm.

Kayo opened his case. 'Please take what you need, process the stone and label it.'

'No problem.'

Kayo took a flashlight and his UltraLite ALS torch from the case and put them in the back pocket of his loose-fitting tan combat trousers. He slid ALS goggles onto his forehead and picked up his digital SLR camera. 'Mensah, are you done?'

'Yes. No prints.'

'Fine, please put it back in position and stand by me. Garba, please pick up the case and come here too.' Kayo took six pictures from three positions then tapped Garba's elbow. 'Could you take measurements of the distances between the boundary pieces of evidence?'

Garba frowned. 'Boundary?'

'The far ends: north, south, east and west.'

Garba nodded.

'After that, bag everything according to their numbers. Mensah, let's go inside.' Kayo suppressed a wave of nausea as he crossed the threshold of the hut with Mensah. The foul smell brought water to his eyes and he blinked. He took the flashlight out of his pocket and swept the inside of the hut with its beam. The floor was marked with the imprint of police boots. Kayo was mildly irritated, but having seen the trail of footprints leading to the hut he wasn't surprised.

To his left there was a pot covered by a calabash, some folded cloth on the floor by the pot, then a mat-covered window opposite the doorway. Also on the floor was a mat with a raised mass on it, which he assumed to be the remains. To the right, on a low table with a short stool beside it, were some foodstuffs: two tubers of yam, a pile of tiny onions, some ginger root, and a miniature basket of tomatoes that had begun to rot. An empty enamel plate and two cooking pots were stored beneath the table. Kayo put the flashlight back in his pocket and put on his ALS goggles. He set the wavelength on the ALS torch to 450 nanometres and scanned the room, only detecting bodily fluids near the entrance and around the remains in the middle of the room. There was no blood splatter. He took off the goggles and pinched a section of the mud floor near the hut's entrance. It smelled like ammonia. Urine. 'Mensah, what do you think this is?'

The other man smelled it. 'Piss,' he said, frowning. 'How did you know it was there?'

Kayo passed the ALS goggles and torch to Mensah.

'Heh, everything is blue blue. I can see the piss. From the mouth of the door, halfway to the mat. This thing is good paa.'

Kayo laughed. 'It's called blue merge technology, but I call it green money technology – expensive. Please measure the length of the trail.'

'Sure.'

Working in silence, Kayo and Mensah tagged all the items in the room and took measurements. Kayo fitted a filter he had made himself to his camera lens and photographed the ALS torch images. He was aware that he was putting off having to deal with the remains on the mat, but he told himself that he needed to process all the surrounding details anyway. He hadn't been on a crime scene for over a year and he wasn't sure that he would feel the same ease. Eventually, he asked Mensah to lift the mat covering the window so he could take pictures of the inside of the hut in natural light to provide control images for the ones he had taken using the camera's flash.

In the bright sunlight, Kayo saw flies scattering from the remains. When he moved closer it was clear that there were maggots embedded in the red mass. They were housefly maggots, but he wasn't sure what strain so it was hard for him to tell how long they had been there. He thought the hunter, Opanyin Poku, might be able to help. Kayo nodded to himself, took a close-up photograph of the mass and stood up. 'Mensah, could you please call the hunter?'

*

I was under the tweneboa tree when he sent for me, the *graduate*, the one they call Kwadwo. He sent the tall red *policeman* with the red eyes to bring me to Kofi Atta's hut. The tall red *policeman*, the Ga man, the one they call Mensah, had been in our village for three nights, watching over Kofi Atta's hut like an owl, and smoking. He didn't talk to anyone, but, always, his red eyes were roaming around the village. Every morning they sent another *policeman* in a car to come and watch Kofi Atta's hut and the red one would sleep in a *tent* beside the hut. That's why when the *graduate* Kwadwo came, I was surprised. I had thought that there was no longer a tale to tell. I mean, sɛbi, I overheard Sargie saying he was coming on dwowda, but on dwowda a fat bald *policeman* came to watch Kofi Atta's hut while the red one slept. Benada too, the same. So wukuda, I didn't even think about it, but if I had looked well I would have seen the signs, the way when I went to forest the ants were finding shelter as though it would rain soon. I mean, the day had gone forward paa when he sent for me, Kwadwo, the *graduate*. It was afternoon and still it hadn't rained. Sebi, later I would know why, but at that time I didn't think about it.

Ei, Kwadwo; you could tell his mother taught him well. When he came he greeted me as a senior man (not like that Sargie). He called me Egya, then he asked to meet our chief and beg leave to look at Kofi Atta's hut and speak to our people. Nana Sekyere received him well and gave him leave to do, sebi, what was needed to put Kofi Atta's case to rest. Hmm. It's true that on our way to Nana Sekyere I saw those three young men carrying some wood for Oforiwaa's father and there I was afraid he would ask about them, but he was looking at the ground. The three of them have grown so strong and muscular; they are the strongest men in the village, but how do we do the job of explaining their existence? That is what was worrying me, but I think Kwadwo was thinking about what to say to Nana Sekyere. I swear on my leg, the way he spoke it was as if he had lived here all his life. Ei Kwadwo! That is why they say that the way the crab lives by the stream makes it understand the ways of water.

So I was under the tweneboa tree when he sent for me, this Kwadwo whose mother was from Kibi. When I got to Kofi Atta's hut, the mouth had changed; I said Ei. The obsidian from the water pot was gone, the bidie was also gone and two chickens were scratching in the sand. There, I raised the kete and went inside. I could still smell Kofi Atta's palm wine (it smelled like akpeteshi now – very strong), but what I saw was wondrous. This *graduate*, Kwadwo, and the *policeman*, Mensah, had put markers, small bright ones with numbers written on them, all over the hut. Everything had a number, even, sebi, the thing on Kofi Atta's kete.

The sun was in the room and Kwadwo was on his knees beside, sɛbi, the thing that looked like a newborn otwe. It is true that I didn't know what to call it so I called it the thing (even when speaking to my wife, Mama Aku, I called it the thing because I had never seen such a thing before). As the wise ones say it is not a name that changes the nature of an animal. When I looked at Kwadwo's hands he was carrying a tiny bottle and something he called *tweezers*. He signalled me to come closer so I walked around the small markers to stand by him. He had a big case open with many wondrous things in it but he raised the tiny bottle he was holding to me so I couldn't look for long. Inside the bottle was a fat, white worm, the kind that become wansima.

He shook my hand. Opanyin Poku, have you seen one of these before?

Ah, this one, I see some all the time. They are from the wansima.

He nodded and pointed at the thing. There were hundreds of the fat, white worms roaming in the redness of it. So, how many days is it before these worms look like this?

I kneeled beside him to look closer.

And there he said: Not too close, it stinks.

But I said: It doesn't stink at all.

He frowned. Oh, I see.

I waited for him to say more but he made quiet, staring at the kɛtɛ. So I said, I've seen these creatures in dead animals after about three days. If it had gone on kraa, four days.

He shook his head and whispered to himself in English. *Was it alive?*

I tapped his shoulder. Have you found something?

He shook his head, then he turned to the door where the tall red *policeman* was standing. *Based on what* Opanyin Poku said, *the life stage of the maggots suggests that this thing might have been alive when it was found.*

The tall red one said: *Impossible Kayo. That's impossible.*

Kwadwo laughed. *I don't know. Experience has taught me that improbable is a better word. Come and help me.* And there he took a bag off his back and removed those bottles that they put hot *tea* in some, and a small box in the same colour, and put them beside him.

The tall red *policeman*, Mensah, came to squat in front of us and Kwadwo passed him an *injection*, the ones the *doctors* use, some small small clear bottles and said *fluid samples*. He, Kwadwo, took a thin knife, sliced little pieces of the thing and put them into some bottles with white covers. The two of them were both wearing *gloves*, but after they put the *samples* in the bottles Kwadwo wore some *specs* like that and opened the bottle that they put hot *tea* in. That's when I saw that there are still things to see in this world! What Kwadwo poured from that *tea* bottle was smoke. He put some of the small small bottles with the *samples* in the box that looked like the *tea* bottle and poured some of the smoke over them. The smoke began to boil before it settled and he closed the box. Then he asked Mensah to pass him something and he opened two bottles with the thing's liquid in them and took a little of each to put on some *glass* that was as thin as a banana leaf. He also put some on paper. Some little pieces you couldn't write your name on. I thought he had forgotten about me, but he turned and said they were just doing some tests. When we finish he said, we should be able to do something about this thing. He pointed at the kɛtɛ.

I said yoo, and asked him what the paper and *glass* were for.

For some *chromatography* tests, not anything big, and some work with the *microscope*. He pointed at a *tube* in the big case.

I said yoo again and kept quiet because I didn't understand what he was talking about, but I knew I would ask him later. I just watched him and Mensah; they used waters and papers that changed colours, and Kwadwo wrote in a *notebook* the colour of cassava leaves. He reminded me of Oduro, our medicine man, who sits in his hut grinding leaves and barks and waters from plants to make drinks and soaps and creams to cure the sick. Nobody watching Oduro can tell what he is doing, but we all go to him. We believe in him. That's how I felt watching this Kwadwo whose mother was from Kibi, where there is gold under the forest.

So I was there (I was thinking about my palm wine) when Kwadwo finished and took *photos* with his *camera*, asked Mensah to take the box that looked like the *tea* bottle to Accra for further *analysis* and sent the other *policeman*, Garba, to ask Oduro how to dispose of the thing. This action that Kwadwo took made me see that the boy really has respect. As I said when I started telling this tale, what was in Kofi Atta's hut was not meant to be seen without the right powers, and Oduro is the one who knows about these things. If we wanted to see the tail of this matter that was brought by a woman in a short short skirt with thin legs, Oduro was our best guide. That is why I was glad when this Kwadwo asked Oduro for advice.

The other *policeman*, Garba, came back running and shouted as soon as he got inside the hut. E say we for burn am before the sun go go ooh.

And there Kwadwo looked up. Garba?

Sorry, sah, *he said we should burn the remains before the sun disappears.*

Garba, *I don't care whether you speak pidgin, Twi or English. I'm trying to find out why you are running.*

It is true that the man looked scared. His hands were as

restless as the wansima that were in the hut. I could tell that this Garba (tall tall and dark, from the north) believed in the old ways so he held on to Oduro's word. Oh sah, e reach four o'clock already. Sun go go down right now noo.

OK, what else the man talk?

E say . . . He turned to me (the Garba one). Opanyin Poku, you know Asare im farm?

Yes. I know am well well.

E say if we pass Asare im farm, before you go reach the kapok for Nana Sekyere im place, you go see two prɛkɛsɛ trees for left, then three kwaseadua for right wey sapow dey grow for top.

I nodded. (I knew the place. It wasn't far from where my mother, sɛbi, had her farm.) Some road dey right side for kwaseadua back.

Ehee! The Garba one nodded. Sweat had come to his face now, so he was glistening like a fish. E say make we no take that road. E say we for pass inside the prɛkɛsɛ then walk small. We go see some *bamboo* for there – big ones. We for enter there.

There, Kwadwo got up. What we dey wait? Garba, come help me plus the thing. Opanyin, will you come with us, to show the way?

So I watched them roll the thing inside the mat like a *cigarette*. Kwadwo took another *photo* and said: *No leakage, interesting*; then we left. The sun was already dipping low, and as we walked I saw the birds flying off to their homes in the redness of the sky. It was as though they had fire in their wings; aburuburu, hornbills, swallows, akroma and sunbirds all in flame like the crackles that fly off my wife's coal pot when she fans the fire hard. At this time, if you went home the women and children would be gathered round the fire. That shows that we had spent a long time in Kofi Atta's hut. (I hadn't even listened to my radio since the Garba *policeman* arrived with Kwadwo. I'm sure *Sunrise FM* played some Jewel Ackah – I like that man's music.) My mother used to tell me that it was good to finish your business before the sun sets, because then the sunset was not the end of the day, but the beginning of the night.

So the sun was dipping low when we set off to look for the *bamboo* trees Oduro sent us to. I remember looking at the sky and saying that the bats would soon take over the air with their blindness.

*

Kayo and Garba listened to Opanyin Poku as he led them towards the edge of the village. They each held one end of the rolled mat carrying the remains from Kofi Atta's hut. Opanyin Poku pointed out how close Kofi Atta lived to Kwaku Wusu, the village's palm-wine tapper, and laughed. Just beyond the palm-wine tapper's hut, on their right, was Asare, the farmer's hut, and then a well-worn path that led to a gap in a short, greening fence that led to the outskirts of the village, past Asare's farm towards the chief's court.

Kayo hadn't noticed the fence the first time he had walked past to see the chief, but now Opanyin Poku explained that the fence was erected from kaagya, a plant that scared snakes and also held fires back.

'That's what we have used for the boundaries of Nana Sekyere's court,' added the old man.

Kayo nodded and scanned either side of the path, trying to take in detail that he hadn't noted before. There were four huts closer to the boundary fence than Kofi Atta's. Three of them, Kwaku Wusu's, Asare's and the hunter's, he surmised were there because their inhabitants worked in the farm or forest, like Kofi Atta did, but he didn't know who lived in the fourth. He quickened his steps to catch up with Opanyin Poku,

71

forcing Garba, who was holding the other end of the rolled mat, to move faster too. 'Opanyin, who lives in that hut beside yours?'

'Oh, there, did you see the girl that came out singing when you arrived? Ehee. That's her home. Her father is the carpenter. He made the stool you saw in Kofi Atta's hut.'

'Mmm. It's a good stool.' Kayo smiled. He mulled over what he knew of the case so far and what was required of him. He was almost certain – even in the absence of corroborative results from the lab in Accra – that the remains were not after-birth, and he was absolutely sure that there had not been a violent crime. Something had died, that was indisputable, but he didn't know what to do about it. Of course, he was going to analyse the evidence that they had collected and establish a timeline and some idea of what had happened in the hut, but what was crucial now was to find out what the people of the village knew. His scientific curiosity was alive to the many oddities of the case. For a start, if the remains weren't after-birth, what were they?

'Left here.' The hunter pointed to a gap in the forest brush between two tall trees – about forty-five feet high, with dense shafts of yellow-green flowers hanging down, emitting a smell that was reminiscent of honey and overripe mangoes.

Kayo felt dizzy as they trudged through the gap and shook his head to clear it. He spotted the circle of bamboo trees as soon as they emerged in the clearing on the other side of the prekɛsɛ trees. It was a high and wide copse – about eight metres wide – covered in weaver bird nests that made the ends of the bamboo shoots bend like burdened vagrants. The plants were tightly packed together and Kayo could see no way of getting to the middle, as instructed by Oduro, without cutting some of the stems.

Opanyin Poku said that if Oduro hadn't asked them to cut

anything then they shouldn't. 'When he speaks, he has spoken,' the hunter insisted.

Garba dropped his end of the rolled mat and turned away, exhaling hard.

Kayo squatted beside the mat and watched Garba walk away.

Suddenly, the tall policeman stopped and exclaimed. 'I see am. I see the way.' He pointed at what seemed to be another closed section of the circle of trees.

Kayo walked up to Garba and saw a path cut at an acute angle into the trees. Kayo slipped between the bamboo and followed the path. The circle was at least twenty trees deep, and the path was cut in a zigzag pattern so that the circle looked closed from a distance. The ground was soft and dark, and it compacted underfoot with each step he took. Halfway in he turned back to rejoin Garba and Opanyin Poku.

The three men walked into the middle of the circle together, with Opanyin Poku leading, Kayo and Garba following with the rolled mat. The earth was covered in yellowed grass and a felled fan palm lay in the centre of the flat area, glowing beside its stump in the last dregs of sunlight.

Garba clapped. 'Ehee, e say make we burn am for the tree im bottom, then bring the top come village.'

Kayo was mildly perturbed at the way everything seemed to have been prepared for them. The path into the bamboo circle was old, but the palm looked freshly chopped. Besides, he had rarely seen a palm growing alone; there was usually another one within yards. Kayo sighed, shrugged and looked towards Garba. 'You mean burn it on the stump?'

'Yes sah.'

Kayo took his notebook from his pocket. He noticed that Opanyin Poku had positioned himself some distance from them and had folded his arms. 'Opanyin, is everything OK?' Kayo tore a page from the notebook.

'Everything is fine, Kwadwo. I'm just letting you do your work. As for me I came to show the way.'

'OK.' Kayo bent over the stump, crumpled the paper in his hand and stuffed it in a hollow in the middle of the stump.

Garba tossed Kayo a lighter.

Kayo paused and inclined his head. 'Garba, is the tree heavy?'

Garba lifted one end of the felled palm. His eyes bulged from his face as he said, 'It's heavy papa!'

'We might have to drag it back,' Kayo concluded.

When the mat caught fire, Kayo and Garba had to jump back; the flame leaped as though the mat had been doused in kerosene. Slowly, a thick white smoke engulfed the entire circle, infusing the air with the smell of nutmeg, honey and thyme. There was a sound of flapping wings, which made Kayo start because he had spotted no birds in the nests around the bamboo trees. When the smoke cleared Kayo found that Opanyin Poku was standing around the stump with them. They were like three points of a triangle around the stump area. The mat and its contents had burned to white ash along with the stump. It was as though the stump had never been there. Garba was smiling, and the last intense redness of the sunset had coloured his hair, making him look like an apparition. Kayo felt light-headed. As he looked up to catch the light, it began to drizzle. 'We'd better leave,' he said.

Opanyin Poku nodded.

Garba went to lift the felled palm and Kayo watched, bemused as the constable hoisted the entire trunk, with its leafy branches, onto his shoulder and headed towards the zigzag path.

*

The village was alight with charcoal fires. The families sat in front of their huts talking, laughing and fanning the flames

74

beneath their cooking food. Kayo pondered the darkness and dry earth that they had encountered outside the copse of bamboo trees. The village didn't seem to have had any precipitation either. The Land Rover Defender was parked near the tweneboa tree at the centre of the village, so Kayo knew Mensah was back. He was relieved; he wanted to go back to Accra soon so that his parents wouldn't be too worried. He had tried his mobile phone on arriving at the village but there was no signal.

Garba dropped the palm outside Kwaku Wusu's hut as instructed by Oduro, and brushed his sullied hands on his uniform.

Opanyin Poku walked with Kayo and Garba to Kofi Atta's hut and asked them if they would come for a drink of palm wine at Akosua Darko's place.

'Oh, yes!' said Garba.

'I don't think so,' countered Kayo. 'I want to get back to Accra to do some work.'

'Oh, sah,' Garba smiled. 'Weytin you fit do this night? It's already seven o'clock.'

'Let's just get the things together.' Kayo stooped to lift the mat that covered Kofi Atta's doorway. A flock of weaver birds flew out, startling him with their cries and frantic flight. He jumped back, still holding the mat, and watched the grey cloud of their progress shift across the sky towards Asare's farm.

Garba laughed, slapping his own stomach as he did so. 'Ei, wonders never end.'

Opanyin Poku remained silent and unperturbed, with a hint of a smile on his face.

Kayo wondered briefly about Garba's demeanour, then entered the hut. He reached into his pocket to grab his flashlight. A quick scan of the floor assured him that nothing in the hut had been touched, except that there was a single blue feather lying in the centre of the floor, where the remains had

75

been. Kayo picked up the feather and took it outside to Opanyin Poku. 'Opanyin, do you know what bird this is from?'

'Mm.' Lines gathered on the hunter's brow.

'What's wrong?'

'Oh, nothing. But, most times, this bird is only seen in Atewa. It's a bee eater. We respect it because it eats that which stings.'

'I see.' Kayo took the feather back and slid it between the pages of his notebook.

Garba put his hand on Kayo's shoulder. 'Sah, you see, there are more things to discover here. Let's stay and leave in the morning.'

Kayo smiled. 'You are just asking because of the palm wine.'

'No, sah, it's because I know the road; it's not good at night – no lights, no reflective road markings.'

'You are coming to drink,' Opanyin Poku stated solemnly.

Kayo raised his head and sighed. 'Garba, could you radio headquarters to send a message to my parents?'

Garba's entire body shook with mirth. 'Oh, sah, this car no radio dey inside. They gave you a small-boy car; not like the one we arrested you with. That one has radio, satellite, CD-changer, TV, manicure, pedicure, parliament . . .'

Kayo laughed in spite of himself. 'OK, let's go and drink. Tomorrow I will insist on a big-man car.'

The drinking spot, or Akosua Darko's place, as the hunter called it, was lit with fire torches that threw multiple shadows against the wall. The constant motion of the dark outlines gave the impression that one was in a crowded room. Kayo blinked as he sat down, trying to adjust to the dimness.

A voluptuous woman, who Kayo estimated to be about forty, came up to them. She was wearing a simple slip dress that emphasised her curves, with a length of green and blue wax print cloth tied around her waist. She introduced herself as

Akosua and asked what they would like. 'As for Opanyin Poku, I know what he wants already,' she joked.

'I'm only here for a short time,' the hunter said. 'I have to go home; Mama Aku has cooked banku.'

Akosua laughed. 'Opanyin, everybody comes here for a short time, but you're the only one who always says it.'

'That's because I'm the oldest man in this village.'

'Oh, as for you!' She turned to Kayo and Garba.

Garba ordered bushmeat soup with palm wine; Kayo simply ordered palm wine.

The woman smiled, revealing deep dimples, and walked away, her hips swaying so harmoniously that Kayo found himself nodding his head to an imaginary beat.

Out of nowhere, Oduro appeared to sit by them. He shook their hands, starting with the hunter who was furthest right, progressing towards his left as was traditional, and ending with Kayo, who held Oduro's hand for much longer than the others did. Oduro was bare-chested, and wore a string of leopard claws around his neck. Kayo thought he was very simply adorned compared to the medicine men he had seen portrayed on television.

Oduro put his hand on the worn wood of their table and leaned forward so his face was close to Kayo's. 'So, sɛbi, the work you went to do; how did it go?'

'It was all right, but there are still many things I don't understand.'

'It is not everything we can understand, my friend.' Oduro rubbed his palms together and sat down. 'Tell me, how do you tell when a man is lying?'

'Well, we use lie detectors.'

'No, no, but why do those things work?'

'Oh, because the body reacts . . . something happens to the body when we lie.'

'You see? That is the matter. How can one understand why the body does that?'

'I don't know.'

Akosua arrived with their palm wine and placed the calabashes on thin sections of bamboo that kept them from tipping before filling them. She had a calabash for Oduro even though he had not yet ordered one. 'I hope you will enjoy the drink.' She nodded at Kayo and Garba. 'Your friend has arrived.' She pointed at an isolated silhouette in a corner of the room.

'It's Mensah,' Garba said. 'I'll go and call him.'

Kayo looked up at the woman, thinking that if she were younger he would have liked to know her a lot better. On a whim, he asked her to taste his palm wine for him.

'Why?' She asked with a twinkle in her eye. 'Am I your wife?'

'No, I just want to learn the correct way to hold the calabash.'

Akosua tasted the wine and passed Kayo's calabash back to him.

'Now I will have to keep this calabash.' Kayo held the calabash under the table with both hands, then raised it with his left as though drawing water from a pot. He took a sip of the wine. 'This is wonderful.'

Akosua smiled and turned to leave.

Opanyin Poku leaned across to touch Kayo's arm. 'Heh, kwadwo nkomodε, she has a daughter, so let your tongue be patient.'

Kayo laughed. 'I'm not a sweet talker so don't call me nkomodε.'

Garba returned with Mensah and sat between Kayo and Opanyin Poku.

Mensah shook hands with everyone and sat beside Oduro, opposite Garba.

'Where is my soup?' Garba asked.

Oduro responded without looking up. 'It is coming with

Akosua's daughter right now.' He looked at Kayo. 'You know the lying matter we were talking about?'

'Yes?' Kayo glanced up to catch a glimpse of Akosua's daughter and looked down again, keeping his eyes fixed on the grain of the table.

'Your machine can be understood, so it can be tricked,' Oduro asserted, 'but if you learn to watch a man, you can always tell what he's thinking.'

A band of heat rose on the back of Kayo's neck. He was still thinking of how stunning Akosua's daughter was. 'How?'

'Stillness.'

'How?'

'Kwadwo, a living thing is always moving; if you look close enough, you can even see, sɛbi, the blood moving beneath the skin. So, if you make an effort, and learn how much of that movement makes up a man's stillness, every other movement will tell you something about him.' Oduro smiled and looked Kayo straight in the eye.

Kayo raised his calabash and took a long swig of palm wine.

Oduro undid the knot of cloth at his waist and took out a wooden vial. 'Here.' He held the vial over Kayo's calabash.

Kayo frowned. 'What is it?'

'Oh, just something I made using the bark of hwɛma. It makes the drink stronger.' The medicine man put two drops in his own wine, took a draught and smacked his lips.

Kayo held up his calabash for Oduro to add some of the potion, stirred his palm wine with his finger and drank. He waited for the quantity he had swallowed to settle in his belly and felt, first the comfort in its weight, then the pull of its strength. He licked his lips slowly. 'Egya Oduro, it tastes good! I feel the kick.'

Oduro leaned across the table, grabbed Kayo's shoulders and smiled. 'It is also an aphrodisiac.' Then he laughed, his whole body shaking, and, with it, Kayo's shoulders.

The laughter increased in volume and intensity until Kayo erupted in mirth too. He felt his head getting lighter. The shadows in the room seemed to rise and laugh with them, and the aroma of bushmeat soup reached out and tickled their eyes and noses with peppery fingers. At some point, Kayo was sure that he was floating above the room with Oduro, looking down at the calabashes, people and soup pots, fading and blending into an array of colours and shapes. He heard a distant xylophone outside, melodious, riding the wind like a charm, splitting the night into slats.

yawda

MORNING HAD BARELY BROKEN WHEN KAYO AND GARBA SET off for Accra. Mensah said he would wait for Sergeant Ofosu to send a vehicle for him, so they left him lying, fully clothed, in his tent. Opanyin Poku, the hunter, had already gone into the forest, but Oduro stood by the tweneboa tree at the village centre, waving benevolently as they pulled into the road. Kayo fell into a pensive silence while Garba hummed another of those overplayed radio songs that Kayo had come to detest. In a way Kayo was glad they had a 'small-boy car'; with Garba's new-found levity Kayo was certain the constable would be blasting music from the radio otherwise.

After a night in Sonokrom, the sounds of the city jolted Kayo as they hit the slow-moving traffic of Adenta. It was only 6:43 a.m. when they got to the outskirts, but with all the professionals of Accra buying property in the new estate developments of the Legon-Madina-Adenta area, the rush-hour traffic had become legendary. Nii Nortey, who had recently moved to the area, claimed that he left home at 5:30 a.m. to avoid the worst of the traffic. Of course, Nii Nortey also used the traffic as an excuse to drink after work, in order to 'let the traffic clear', he insisted. Kayo smiled, pulled his mobile phone out of one of his many pockets and glanced at it – 7:02 a.m. In the midst of the blaring horns and cheerful cross-lane banter of taxi drivers, Kayo was aware that he hadn't confirmed his results. A number of the tests he had done in Kofi Atta's hut were improvised, so he needed to double-check the outcomes before they got to P. J. Donkor's residence. He dialled his office number at Acquabio and waited for the hollow, single-tone ring at the other end.

Joseph picked up on the fourth ring.

Kayo was relieved that his intuition was right. 'Good morning, Joseph.'

'Oh, Boss!' Joseph exclaimed, then lowered his voice. 'Mr Kayo, what happened? Mr Acquah told us that you stole money and left, but I didn't believe him. You will not leave us like that. Also I told the technicians. You would never just leave. Also Eunice said there was a police sergeant in the matter. Sir—'

'Joseph.' Kayo had never heard Joseph speak so much but he didn't have the time to indulge him. 'Is someone in the office?'

'No sir, sorry, Mr Kayo, just me.'

'OK. Did the policeman, Constable Mensah, come to you with the samples?'

'Yes, Mr Kayo.' Joseph's voice was still low, conspirational.

Kayo took out his notebook and pen and leaned on the dashboard in front of him to write. He wrote *Afterbirth*, *Animal*, and *Human* in a horizontal line and drew boxes around the words. 'Did you find the book in my drawer to help with the tests?'

'Yes, Mr Kayo, I did them all yesterday, the tests. I stayed after six. Also I put a report on a disk for you.'

'No time for that now, Joseph. Somebody will come for the disk, but I need some details first.'

'OK.'

'Tell me, did you detect any meconium in any of the samples?'

'No sir.'

Kayo crossed out *Afterbirth*. 'Was the blood human?'

'Type O.'

'Excellent.' Kayo lowered his voice as he drew a fine line through *Animal*, glancing at Garba from the corner of his eye. 'Did they – the constable – did he . . .'

'Oh yes, Mr Kayo, they paid me. Thank you. Even more than my monthly pay.'

'Good.' Kayo closed his notebook and put the pen beside it.

'Oh, Mr Kayo?'

'Yes.'

'When are you coming back?'

Kayo smiled, switching the mobile phone from his left to his right hand. 'I don't know.' He paused and swallowed the saliva that seemed to have pooled in his mouth. 'Bye Joseph.'

'Bye.'

Kayo slipped the phone into his pocket and leaned back, adjusting the seat the same way he had on the way to Sonokrom. It was easier this time. When he looked to his side Garba was smiling. They had just passed the University of Ghana campus at Legon, heading in the direction of Accra Central.

Garba tapped Kayo's knee, smiling. 'So, Mr Kayo, are you ready for Donkor?'

'I thought you were supposed to call him by his title.'

'Oh, Mr Kayo, we know where these men shit. Don't mind Ofosu; he tries to look big. He thinks he's the only sergeant in the police force.' Garba honked the Land Rover's horn cheerfully as a Peugeot 504 appeared to stall in front of them. 'Seriously, Mr Kayo, we reach Donkor im there finish; everything fine or make I delay small?'

'Oh, I'm fine thank you.' Kayo looked to his left where, beyond Garba's head, the nouveau riche community of East Legon sat, spreading like melting lard in the still rising sun. That was where many of his peers aspired to live and they worked towards it with a conscience-free zeal, cheating and bribing where necessary. He picked up his notebook and put it in his lap. 'Where does P. J. Donkor live?'

'Airport,' Garba replied. 'We just cross Tetteh Quarshie Roundabout, then fourth junction on the right. He lives around there.'

Kayo nodded. Airport was one of the most expensive neighbourhoods in Accra, and, although Kayo didn't understand why anyone would pay more money to live close to the sound of aeroplanes, he didn't think it was possible to afford Airport on a police inspector's salary.

Garba pulled up outside an elaborate burgundy gate flanked by high cream walls, and honked his horn. Kayo noticed a huge satellite dish on the part of the roof that wasn't obscured by the gate, no doubt the channel for Inspector Donkor's fixation with *CSI*. A policeman's head appeared in a small window punched out of the wall of a tiny guardroom to the right of the gate. Garba gave a thumbs-up and another policeman emerged to open the gate.

P. J. Donkor's courtyard was designed like a hotel driveway, with a semicircular path that led to the entrance. Garba drove to the middle point of the semicircle, where P. J. Donkor stood flanked by two white Roman pillars and a policewoman holding a tray with two glasses of a yellow-orange juice. The house, like the external walls, was cream, accentuated by white window frames, doors and fixtures. Garba got out, took off his cap and stood to attention by Kayo's door, facing the inspector as Kayo stepped out of the car.

'Good morning, sah,' Garba barked.

The inspector smiled with his tiny teeth and said, 'At ease, Constable. I see you have brought my man.'

'Yes, sah.'

'Anything to report?' P. J. Donkor still had the remains of a smile on his face.

'No sah.'

The inspector jerked his head upwards and Garba walked swiftly to the driver's side of the Land Rover.

Kayo turned to Garba, wondering if the constable was going off with all his equipment. 'Where you dey go?'

Garba slid into the vehicle. 'I'm going to refuel and come and take you home.'

'Oh, OK.' Kayo bent to speak through the passenger window. 'Can you change this car and get one with parliament?'

Garba laughed, adjusting his cap as he pulled away.

'Ah, Mr Kayo.' The inspector addressed Kayo as though he'd just seen him. 'Please come with me.'

The policewoman with the tray headed left. The inspector and Kayo followed. The inspector was wearing a burgundy dressing gown with *PJD* embroidered above the left breast and a sepow symbol on the back.

Kayo tried to remember where he had last encountered the word sepow – the wicked sepow.

'So what is this car with "parliament" business with Garba?' Inspector Donkor's eyes sparkled with intensity.

'Oh, it was a joke. The car you sent us with had no air conditioning or radio, so I wanted him to get a better-equipped car.'

Inspector Donkor laughed, stopping to stamp his slipper-clad feet on the polished granite floor as they reached his verandah. The policewoman had placed the tray on a white table with two chairs facing Inspector Donkor's swimming pool.

Kayo reached out to turn one of the chairs around to face the other, but the inspector placed a hand on his shoulder.

'It's easier to talk when we can contemplate nature.' His cheek twitched as he ushered Kayo into the seat on the right, then he pointed at the tray that the policewoman had left before disappearing. 'Shall we have some orange juice?'

Kayo raised a glass and took a cautious sip.

Inspector Donkor drained his glass in one smooth action, sighed and smacked his lips. 'So, my young *CSI* man, how was Sonokrom? Give me the raw facts you uncovered.' He leaned back and stared at the surface of the swimming pool.

'Well, the remains were not afterbirth as the initial report suggested, but they are definitely human.' Kayo looked at Inspector Donkor, but the man was motionless and seemed to have no intention of interrupting. Kayo found it odd speaking to someone he couldn't look in the eye, but he carried on. 'There didn't seem to be any external interference since the fingerprints we got from inside the hut where the remains were found were very consistent, all from the same person. I'm assuming that they are all from the cocoa farmer who lived in the hut, Kofi Atta, who everyone claims not to have seen for weeks. Most of them say about a month.' Kayo glanced sideways at Inspector Donkor again, exhaling. He had considered that Kofi Atta could have killed someone and brought the remains into the hut, but Kayo didn't want to explore that possibility quite yet. No one else was missing from the village.

Apart from two twitches of the cheek Inspector Donkor showed no reaction.

Kayo couldn't tell the inspector about the sweet smell of the flesh they burned, or about the birds that had left their nests in the bamboo to fill an empty hut, so he had nothing worth telling him. Kayo was caught in a void between instinct and knowledge and, for once in his professional life, he didn't have the answers.

Inspector Donkor sat up suddenly. 'So, if the remains aren't afterbirth, who are they? I mean, who is it?' His voice was controlled but his impatience was obvious.

'Well, Inspector, for specific answers like that I need to finish analysing some samples in Accra and interview some of the villagers. The truth is right now . . .' Kayo shifted in his chair. 'I mean it could be Kofi Atta, it could be a victim of his. What I do know is, whatever the case, there was no violence in the hut.'

Inspector Donkor brought his palms together and rested his chin on his thumbs as though he was praying. He inhaled, then stood up abruptly, slapping the white table in front of him with his palm. Kayo caught his own glass before the juice spilled, but Inspector Donkor's glass teetered on the edge of the table, then dropped to the granite floor and shattered.

The inspector didn't seem to notice the glass breaking. His eyes were wild as he yelled. 'I woke up for you, young man. 6 a.m. for you. And I'm not interested in whether there was a violent crime or not, I need this to be a big case. Do you understand?' He put his right index finger on the table as though he was crushing a bug.

Kayo put his glass back on the table, moving slowly. When he had bent to catch it a dark shape beneath the inspector's chair had caught his eye. It looked like a gun strapped in a makeshift holster. Kayo didn't want to take any chances. 'I'm only telling you what I can say for certain right now. It will take me a few days to get to the truth.'

Inspector Donkor drummed a metronomic rhythm on the table with his finger. 'I am not interested in the truth. I am interested in results. Do you understand? I need you to make this a big case with international implications.' He sat back in his chair.

Kayo stood up. He was apprehensive, but he couldn't let the inspector change the rules when the job was in progress; he was destined to fail if that happened. 'With all due respect, that wasn't what we agreed. You said some minister was interested in the results, and I have what I need to tell you what happened. I just need to develop a hypothesis based on what I've collected, then you'll have your report.'

Inspector Donkor rose and held Kayo's eyes. 'Look Mr Kayo; are you stupid or just stubborn? Do you realise I can send you straight back to prison for your conspiracy?'

Kayo didn't even bother to question the so-called conspiracy. He sat back down and stared beyond the pool, at a fine, trimmed row of hedges, in front of which a pigeon was scratching for worms. He realised now why Sergeant Ofosu had been so amused when he tried to question the authority by which he was arrested. These men allowed you access to your rights according to their whims; the inspector had no intention of honouring the promise that he had made in his office; Kayo was only guaranteed freedom as long as he made sure Inspector Donkor got what he wanted.

Inspector Donkor put his right arm around Kayo. 'Look, I want us to work well together. I want you to go back to the village; don't return until you have a good scientific theory and report – *CSI*-style.' He reached across with his left hand and held Kayo's chin up with his fingers. 'Do you think you can do that for me?'

Kayo exhaled, extricated himself from Inspector Donkor's hold, and stood. 'Well, you didn't track me down for the length of my legs, did you?'

Inspector Donkor laughed heartily. 'Ei, this young man. One day in the village and you want to riddle me with proverbs.' He slapped Kayo's shoulder. 'Come and let me show you around the house before Garba comes back. But you can't see the master bedroom because my wife is still sleeping.' The inspector winked and motioned for Kayo to follow him.

The policewoman who had shown them to the verandah appeared from nowhere with a servant boy and instructed him to clean up the shattered glass.

*

Kayo barely had time to pass his new samples – a couple of swabs for PCR tests – on to DC Mensah, then go home and pack some clothes, his laptop and his three extra batteries before he was on the road again with Garba. Kayo's younger brother, Kakra, was at home. He had left his National Service teaching job in Kintampo for a long weekend because they hadn't been given their allowance for two months. Garba got out of the car as soon as he heard the word Kintampo, excited because he said his family lived there. He shook Kakra's hand vigorously and riddled him with questions.

Kakra was impressed by the car with parliament – a Range Rover with a CD-changer, high radio antenna and air conditioning, but his main preoccupation was convincing Kayo to let him borrow his Golf for the weekend.

Kayo refused initially, but remembered that his mother would need to visit his sister on the university campus on Saturday. 'We have a deal if you promise to drive Ma to visit Esi on Saturday.' Kayo paused, thinking that he had made far too many deals recently that weren't in his favour. 'Deal?'

Kayo's mother had been worried over his absence the last two days. She didn't say so but Kayo could tell by the way she fussed over him, adjusting his shirt and packing fried fish for them to travel with. 'If you didn't love food so much, I would have thought that you had run away,' she joked.

'Then your food must be really good, Auntie, because there is a woman in the village we are working in, I'm telling you . . .' Garba broke off his sentence and shook his head in mock amazement.

'Ei, Kwadwo, but you haven't told me anything about this.'

'Oh Ma,' Kayo threw a stern glance in Garba's direction. He wasn't sure he liked the familiar way the constable interacted with his family. 'Can't you see he's joking? It's just a chop bar.' He headed for the living room to say goodbye to his father.

Once they were clear of traffic, Garba turned the volume down on the radio and turned to Kayo. 'Mr Kayo, you have a nice family.'

Kayo placed his left hand on the dashboard. After their two journeys together he had learned that Garba always preceded his questioning with a statement. He looked at the constable, who had been allowed to wear mufti since he was on assignment with a civilian. 'What do you want to ask, Garba?'

Garba's grin was sheepish. 'Do you have another brother?'

'Why do you ask?'

'Your brother I just met is called Kakra. As far as I know, there is no Kakra without a Panyin.'

'It could have been a girl.'

The constable laughed. 'But it's a boy.'

'He was.' Kayo sighed. 'He died soon after he was born.'

'Oh, sorry Mr Kayo. How old was he? What happened?'

'He choked. We never found out what caused the choking; he looked like he was laughing.' Kayo pushed his back hard against his seat as though he wanted to be absorbed. 'He was only two months old. My grandfather said the baby was just a messenger.'

'Hmm.' Barely audible strains of Egya Koo Nimo's 'Akora Dua Kube' came on the radio and Garba turned the volume up as the veteran musician – a biochemist by training – exhorted young men to put their hands to work.

Kayo gazed at the vast lands to either side of the road, taking in the rich green of the vegetation. He had been amazed to see the varied wealth of the landscape driving up from Accra to Tafo; the hills that appeared to fade into the massed trunks of giant trees, the odd baobab rising like a grey sentinel above smaller trees; and by the sides of the roads life progressing as though modern initiatives were a passing fancy. Children balanced yam, cassava and woven baskets containing tomatoes on their heads, farmers walked bare-chested and barefoot into the shade, with cutlasses swinging at their sides – and every one of them understood the language of the forest; a language Kayo didn't know.

'He is wise, your grandfather.' The Koo Nimo song had ended and Garba had turned the volume back down.

'He was.' Kayo cracked a malnourished smile. 'He died too – exactly one year after the baby.'

'I'm sorry.'

'Don't apologise. We all go die some; no be so?'

Garba nodded with a hesitance that Kayo interpreted as reluctance.

'What about you?' Kayo managed to keep pain from creeping into his voice. 'How big is your family in Kintampo?'

'Oh, ours is simple. Four brothers – we are all boys in the house. Hard men.' Garba laughed as he said 'hard', emphasising his point by clenching his fist, then going on to reveal that two of his brothers worked as policemen in Kumasi, while the eldest worked with his father, training horses. Squinting at the hard sunlight pouring in from the windscreen, he asked Kayo if he had noticed how pretty the policewoman at Donkor's house was.

Kayo smiled but didn't speak.

Garba nodded. 'That Donkor guy is smart. That's his secret weapon. He found out the girl was raped by the deputy chief's son so he hired her to work in his unit. At the time, he was just a sergeant ooh; he had passed his exams, but no promotion. Chale, as soon as he hired that girl, he got inspector; and then, within six months, they gave him this post – PRCC.

He has the powers of a chief superintendent already, or even deputy commissioner, but they have to wait before they make it official. We call him Inspector, but we know.' Garba sighed. 'This earth, my brother.'

Kayo thought about the woman's delicate hands that he had noticed but hadn't questioned. It all made sense now; he had found it incredible that the inspector had a member of the Ghana Police Service waiting on him.

'That's why I want my younger brother to go to university.' Garba tapped Kayo's knee. 'He won't have to struggle like us. Inshallah.'

'Garba, I thought you weren't Muslim.'

'I'm not. Nobody owns Inshallah. I lie?' He broke into laughter again, almost choking this time.

'You no lie.' Kayo smiled and shook his head, noticing how relaxed Garba looked in a cream Lacoste shirt, so different from the intense constable he had driven up with just a day earlier. He was still armed; a pistol was slung across his waist, but he seemed less severe.

Garba coughed. 'Mr Kayo?'

'Yes.'

'Was your grandfather powerful?'

'What do you mean?'

'I mean spiritually.'

'I don't know,' Kayo frowned. 'He was a fisherman. He went to sea.'

'You see, the way he died exactly one year after your brother, I've heard that sometimes the powerful ones have to go and show the way back to the other side.' Garba paused to swerve a pothole in the road. 'You follow me?'

'I'm not sure, can you . . .'

'I mean, maybe Panyin was lost.' Garba shook his head. 'Anyway, you are a book man. I'm sure you don't believe these things.'

'Not really. My grandfather drowned.'

'Ahh, OK.'

They drove in silence until they got to Sonokrom. As they pulled in near the tweneboa tree, Kayo spotted Oduro standing, in almost the same position he was when Kayo and Garba left, with a greying pole-like man beside him. Coming back from the city, Kayo realised that these men were so at ease being bare-chested that, except for Oduro, who stood out because of the leopard claws around his neck, he hadn't taken note of it during his first visit. He wondered, briefly, if he'd missed something as significant about the women.

Oduro walked up to him and shook his hand. 'Kwadwo, welcome back.'

Kayo acknowledged Oduro's welcome and they shook hands.

'This is Sarfo,' Oduro said. 'His grandson just broke his arm.'

Kayo nodded, wondering why he was being introduced.

Oduro pointed at Garba. 'Yesterday night your friend said you're a doctor.'

Kayo tried to remember at what point in the conversation at Akosua Darko's place Garba had said anything about his being a doctor, but the entire night was a collection of fragments in his brain.

'We need your help.' The medicine man started walking towards his hut to the right of the tweneboa tree, signalling for Kayo to follow him. 'You know the child, Kusi. He was one of the children who ran to your car when you arrived yesterday.'

'Oh, the older one.'

The tall greying man, Sarfo, who hadn't said anything before, laughed at this. 'He rather is the youngest. It is his height that makes him look old. He took after me.'

Oduro's hut was at least three times the size of Kofi Atta's. It was flanked by two other huts, and had a fenced area a couple of yards in front of it where a few dozen chickens clucked contentedly. Kayo smiled when he noticed the large patch of corn stalks beside a hut which stood on the other side of the chickens; somebody obviously understood demand and supply.

Inside Oduro's hut, behind a short mud wall, the children who had run to fuss over the Land Rover the day before were standing around a mat on which Kusi lay. The boy was framed in the sunlight streaming in from the window-hole, cradling his right arm and breathing heavily, but he didn't seem to be in pain.

Kayo squatted, put his hand on Kusi's forehead and smiled at him. 'Kusi, how are you? Does it hurt?'

The boy shook his head. 'Egya Oduro rubbed some leaves on it and it stopped paining me.' He moved his left arm to show the broken right arm.

The forearm was bent like a boomerang, such that Kusi's hand seemed to be reaching up towards his chin. Kayo ran his fingers gently, hesitantly, along the arm, applying more pressure as he gripped it to feel for the break. He had only ever studied this in theory and had never dealt with a fracture except in first aid. After a couple of gentle displacements, Kayo concluded that it was just a greenstick fracture and breathed a sigh of relief. He was not equipped to do any invasive work, and he wasn't even sure he would have done a good job if he had to. 'It's good you are young,' he said to the boy, straightening up.

Kayo turned to Oduro, who was leaning over the wall with Garba and Sarfo. 'It's not serious, but we'll need to straighten it and tie it.'

'Oh, Awurade, we thank you,' exclaimed Sarfo.

Oduro nodded. 'Good. I didn't want to touch it because I wasn't sure.'

'Hmm.' Kayo got the feeling he was being tested but he

nodded anyway, then turned to Garba. 'Chale, Garba, can you find some sticks about the length of his arm' – he gestured towards Kusi – 'and bring them to me?'

Oduro put an arm around Kayo. 'My friend, Kwadwo. Have you thought about learning healing with our plants and soils?'

'No.' Kayo put his hands in his pockets. 'But I would like to ask you some questions about Kofi Atta.'

Kayo felt Oduro's arm stiffen on his shoulder before the medicine man patted him on the back. 'Later, Kwadwo, at Akosua Darko's place.' Oduro rubbed his hands together like an illusionist. 'Let me bring you some cloth for tying the arm.'

*

Even in the middle of the day the inside of Akosua Darko's place was murky. Kayo noticed that all the window-holes were covered by raffia mats, which let in little slits of sunlight, but not enough to illuminate the space. The hunter was sitting at the same table he was at the previous night, with what looked like an old Enfield rifle propped up beside him, nursing a calabash of palm wine. As Kayo, Garba and Oduro walked over to join him, two heavily muscled young men in their twenties emerged from the back of the hut where the cooking was done. The sweat on their torsos glistened briefly in the flame from the single fire torch hanging from a hook in the middle of the hut before they slipped out of the main door.

The hunter waved at them. 'Kwadwo, it's good you're back. That day I forgot to tell you; I think you would make a good hunter.'

'Opanyin Poku,' Kayo laughed. Now that he was closer he noted there was no breech on the rifle; it was definitely an Enfield. 'You already told me, and you told this man the same thing.' He pointed at Garba.

'Oh, good. It's true – you both have patience. Patience is

95

the key to good hunting.' He took a sip of his palm wine. 'Can you smell the food?'

Kayo and Garba nodded, shaking the hunter's hand and sitting down opposite him.

'You caught antelope?' Oduro asked as he shook the hunter's hand.

The hunter grabbed his rifle and shook it. 'Eh heh. This long gun of mine, it is effective paa.'

Oduro sat down beside the hunter. 'Your friend here wants to talk about Kofi Atta.'

'I see.' The hunter looked at Kayo and Garba. 'What do you want to know?'

Akosua's daughter came to the table with three drinking calabashes and a larger calabash bearing palm wine. She greeted the men, put calabashes in front of each of them and served them. She topped up Opanyin Poku's calabash and took a step away from the table. 'Would you like to have some fufu with antelope soup? They just finished pounding the fufu.'

Garba said yes immediately, so did Oduro.

'I caught the antelope, so I will eat until, sɛbi, I go crazy,' said the hunter with a toothy grin.

'What is your name?' Kayo asked.

'Esi.' The girl's expression barely changed.

'Esi, yes, I would like some fufu.'

She nodded and walked away.

The men were quiet for a few seconds, then, unexpectedly, Garba spoke. 'About Kofi Atta; we'd like to know what he does, who his friends and relatives are – things like that. Was anyone living with him?'

Kayo turned to Garba, raising his eyebrows. He hadn't thought the constable had been paying attention to the work he was doing at all.

Oduro turned to the hunter who shook his head and looked

at the floor as though he carried an unbearable weight. The sinews of his shoulders pulsed like a clenched jaw.

'I know him well, Kofi Atta, but his character is bad. It doesn't take long for him to get angry.' Opanyin Poku paused to drink some of his palm wine. 'His daughter used to live with him but she left.' He looked up at Kayo. 'Can I tell you one of our old stories? It's about a cocoa farmer, like Kofi Atta.'

'After we finish with Kofi Atta,' Kayo smiled.

'There is not much to tell. He's a cocoa farmer, he was married, his wife died and his daughter left.'

Kayo leaned forward. 'Who were his friends?'

'He didn't have friends; not good friends. Bad character.'

Esi appeared to refill their calabashes and returned to the back of the hut.

Oduro, his mouth still gleaming from his last draught of palm wine, tapped the arm Kayo had rested on the table between them and showed him his wooden vial.

Kayo nodded, then turned to Garba. 'You should try it too. It gives the palm wine a good kick.'

Garba winked at the medicine man and Oduro put a couple of drops in his calabash.

Kayo turned back to Opanyin Poku. 'So, when was the last time you saw Kofi Atta?'

'Less than one moon ago; he was going to his farm early. You know the early cocoa harvest is soon.'

Kayo tried to remember if he had ever been taught about a cocoa harvest that started soon after July, but all he could remember was the main October to January harvest. That's when the Produce Buying Company used to advertise to farmers on TV, even though he didn't think many of the farmers used TVs. He shook his head as if to clear his mind. 'Did he say anything, Kofi Atta?'

'Kwadwo.' The hunter raised a finger to point at Kayo. 'Your questions will live a lot longer than me. We have drunk, and there is meat coming. Let me tell you the story.'

Kayo sighed.

''53.' The hunter pointed again, his finger casting a shadow on the wall behind him. 'That year was unlike other years. I am not a book man like you but you can go and look. The matters, sɛbi, that we have in the world today, many have something to do with that year.' He took a draught of his palm wine. 'Sɛbi, in the tradition of our elders, maybe I will put myself in the story but it is not me, you hear?'

The men nodded. The flame in the centre of the hut, behind Kayo and Garba, was reflected in the hunter's eyes, and on the wall behind Oduro and the hunter, the shadows of the men merged like so many rivers.

*

It was the year after Nkrumah became our land's elder. I mean, sɛbi, the Englishman was still here, but Nkrumah was *prime minister*; he went around visiting villages, greeting the people. Yes, he visited this village (Oduro will bear witness) and many other villages near here. One of these villages, that is where the *cocoa* farmer lived. I mean, it was like this village, but with more trees. Even if you were by the road you couldn't see far – the trees were thick thick. '53 – it was unlike any other year. In that village (let's say that it is called K Krom), Tintin, a royal musician, walked to a church in Tafo because he had heard that they had a new instrument there that played music. They were there when he came running back, screaming like a fowl that somebody was chasing. He said the instrument (he called it *organ*) was evil because it made people stand up – every time the Englishman put his fingers on it everybody would stand up; the music was sweet, but the instrument was cursed.

That same night, the musician, Tintin, disappeared. Everybody thought, sɛbi, he was dead, but I will tell you the truth later. For now, as the wise ones say, one does not turn away from an elephant to throw stones at a small bird. The story I am telling you is the story of the *cocoa* farmer. The night Tintin disappeared, the farmer's wife gave birth to a daughter, Mensisi. Her cry was so loud and it cut through the forest like a matchet. The fires in the village were still lit and glowed in the faces of those waiting for news of the baby. Hmm, it will shock you when I say that nobody was surprised at what happened after the child was born, but '53 was that kind of year.

Right after the birth, when the old ladies had come from the hut to whisper to the *cocoa* farmer that he had a daughter and he had gone off to celebrate with palm wine, the wife died. (Let us drink some wine for those that have gone to the other side.) I mean, all things are in Onyame's wide hands, but it can be said that this death is what started the *cocoa* farmer's troubles.

There was a sound of gentle footsteps. As Kayo turned around to see who was coming, the hunter paused and smiled. Esi stepped through the back doorway of Akosua Darko's bearing a large bowl of water. Her form, barely visible when she was on the other side of the fire torch in the middle of the hut, was clearly framed in silhouette once she got closer to the table. The simple orange and black batik cloth she had wrapped over her breasts was amplified halfway down her body by her hips, which swung with the casual ease of a hypnotist's pendant. She bent over the table, avoiding the calabashes, placed the bowl of water at the centre and stood back, her bare feet dark against the baked mud floor. Kayo could feel the combined effect of the palm wine and Oduro's hwɛma concoction; it made the world feel lighter, unreal.

The hunter put his hands in the bowl to wash them. 'Ah,

time to eat some fufu and meat. The fufu here is the softest I've ever had; ask Oduro.'

Oduro nodded, plunging his right hand in the bowl. Kayo followed suit.

'Your story is interesting,' said Garba, dipping a hand into the bowl. 'I am interested in the musician.'

'Oh, I'll tell you everything; be patient.' The hunter stared at the bowl of water, with all the hands making waves in it, and smiled. 'Ei, this earth,' he exclaimed.

Kayo removed his hand from the water and flicked the droplets onto the ground behind him, away from Esi's feet. 'So, Opanyin. Your cocoa farmer, what is his name?'

Opanyin Poku looked up at Esi, grinned, then turned to Kayo and Garba. 'Let's say his name is Kwaku Ananse.'

Oduro laughed and stamped his feet, and Kayo noticed Esi suppressing a giggle with her hand as she reached over to take the water away. She returned, accompanied by her mother, with earthenware bowls filled with fufu and the richest, reddest palm nut soup Kayo had ever seen. On the surface of the soup were cuts of okro, chillies and garden eggs. Large chunks of antelope meat were submerged like vessels guarding pale cream islands of fufu. The soup was steaming hot.

Akosua lit a torch close to them so that they could see their food, then she put her arm around her daughter's waist and marched her back to the rear of the hut.

Oduro poured a bit of palm wine on the floor and said, 'Our fathers, we share our meal with you.'

The men looked at each other, nodded their heads, and then, as one, dipped their fingers into the red soup.

*

It is no mystery that when something leaves your hand, grief can take its place; it is the same way that rain takes the place of clouds. What we cannot understand is how heavy the rain can be. Hmm. After Kwaku Ananse's wife died he cried paa, hard paa. Indeed many say he never stopped crying. For many moons he slept and rose and never looked at the sky. He wandered to his farm like a creature stunned by gunfire and wandered back again, with his cutlass in his hand. And this cutlass, he didn't even use. His farm grew wild, with sapow, elephant grass, mmofra forowa and nettles growing beneath the *cocoa* trees, covering the earth in the same way his beard covered his face. Oh, and palm wine (you know I don't play with my palm wine), palm wine; he drank palm wine like a river drinks rain. So, as I have said, he went and came like this until his beard and moustache swallowed his mouth. That is when people remembered that he hadn't spoken since his wife died.

So, his mother-in-law, Yaa Somu, went and stood in front of him one morning when he was walking to his farm, took his cutlass and pointed at him.

Kwaku, stop questioning the ancestors and look around you. See grasscutters, aburuburu, wansima; my son, all these creatures die, but the rest carry on. Listen, don't walk around thinking that the Onyame owes you something. You have a beautiful daughter, she has not even seen your face. Stop mourning the dead and take care of the living.

And there she raised the cutlass as though she was going to cut him, and brought it down by his feet. I swear my mother, he didn't even move. Ei!

It is true that those who knew Ananse understood his sadness. Sɛbi, since the time before his penis knew to stand up for the right purpose, he had done everything to get close to his wife. As he matured and learned the ways of the world, he realised, sɛbi, since she grew to be one of the most beautiful girls in the sixteen villages under their chief (I mean she was kama: standing breasts, thick thighs, with a smile that was wider than an embrace. Not one of these thin girls nowadays); he knew he would have competitors for her hand. He needed wealth and he set out to get it. Although he wasn't born to a wealthy man, he was related to the chief, so he went with humility and asked for some land to plant *cocoa*.

Cocoa was a problem crop at the time (about '46), a lot of diseases, so nobody was planting it in our villages. Farmers were still planting cassava and yam and doing well, so Nana wanted to ask him to think about his choice well, but the intensity burning in Ananse's eyes made him turn his heart. This is how Ananse became the only *cocoa* farmer in our villages. They say somebody was looking over him, because that same year the *government* found ways of controlling the diseases. Within two years of his first harvest, Ananse had become a wealthy man and he was married to the woman he had pursued since he was a boy.

So, sɛbi, losing his wife two years after he married her was not an easy thing for Ananse, but, as his mother-in-law, Yaa Somu, said, he had a daughter. I think when he sat down over the matter, he saw that his mother-in-law was right, so he stopped crying.

One morning as I was coming back from forest (I was checking my traps; I had four ndanko) I saw him walking to Yaa Somu's home. He had removed his beard, his moustache, and the long pieces of hair that had grown on his head. He said Agoo, and Yaa Somu came out, still tightening her cloth around her breasts. Ananse went to his knees and begged for forgiveness. Yaa Somu told him to stand up and stop being foolish, and there she went inside and brought the child to him.

She said, You have been in a dark place, but, with your relatives, we outdoored this child for you. Her name is Mensisi.

We will still care for her, but from today she will sleep in your home.

From that day Ananse looked after the girl as if she was a gift. (She wasn't one year when he went for her.) He carried her on his back all the time, when he came back from the farm, he would rush to Yaa Somu's hut to take the girl fruit, and listen to her silly talk while he took her to his home. We were not surprised when she started walking and followed him everywhere. Indeed some of the women in the village said it was unnatural for a man to take such interest in his daughter; they said it was like a love affair.

The wise ones say that everything in this world is like sleep; it comes and goes. It is so with happiness and madness. In this time I'm talking about, a man came from the faraway land of *Kenya* and said he was running from Englishmen who were trying to cut his testicles (the world is wondrous, I'm telling you!); that is when we knew a time of madness had come.

About two years after the one from *Kenya* came, your friend Tintin, the musician, came back. It was with his coming that we saw Ananse's illness.

Mensisi was playing with one of my sons under a palm-nut tree by the goats at the back of the village. They tied the tree with hamabiri and took turns to hold the hamabiri so the other could jump over it (like what you call *high jump*). Mensisi couldn't jump well because she was only about four years, but my son was six years so he could jump. It was about to get dark; the bats had already taken to the skies and the sun, sɛbi, was sending its message to the palm-wine drinkers – those of us who gather to drink before we go home to delve into the mysteries of our wives' pots. The leaves were going dark and those in their homes were making sure they had *krasine* for their fires. But a child doesn't see these things; for them, as long as there is light, it is day.

So, Mensisi was holding the hamabiri when she dropped it and said, What's that?

My son said, What? Why have you dropped the rope?

Listen, she said. It is true that Mensisi knew what she liked even at that age. She started walking towards forest.

My son followed her, and night came.

To see Kwaku Ananse while the children were missing was to see, sɛbi, madness alive. He wanted to do so many things that he couldn't move. He kneeled down beside the palm-nut tree, where they had been playing, and beat the ground. When Yaa Somu went to comfort him, he turned on her and insulted her.

You anyɛn, you didn't watch her. What were you doing? What were you doing? Are you trying to tell me I can't even go to my farm anymore? You are anyɛn. Anyɛn ooh, anyɛn.

Yaa Somu just turned around and left him. She didn't need to speak. We all knew that if she hadn't been there when he was using all his time to cry for his dead wife, the child would have died. And still, even though she was old (older than Ananse's own mother, who was dead), she was the one who cared for the child during the day.

I went to Ananse and told him to be quiet. The best thing would be for me to go with my long gun to find the children and he could wait in the village.

The medicine man (he also was Oduro, like this one) agreed and told Ananse to stop worrying. We are all friends in the sixteen villages, he said. The only danger is from animals, snakes, and I have the best snakebite medicine, so everything will be well.

I followed the children's footprints from the palm-nut tree into the forest. It was dark but there was enough moonlight for me because my eyes are used to dimness; it is the way I hunt. I could smell the grasses and bushes as my skin rubbed against them so I knew where I was.

The children had not found a path so they had stepped on bushes as they walked; in the pale light the path they had walked looked like a muddy river. I had my cutlass as well, so in places where their size had allowed them to pass beneath branches, I was able to cut my way through. (This is when I found that children can't walk straight ooh; they are too curious.) I went left, then right, left, then right; cutting palm, twapea, rough lime, young neem shoots, kyerεkyerεma, gyedua . . . I mean cutting was all I was cutting, and thinking about my son and the little girl, Mensisi, when suddenly I saw a light – a firelight. I crouched in the bushes with my cutlass and long gun and watched. When the light got close to me I saw two tall men, dark, with facial marks (like Garba here), talking. One was carrying the light and the other was carrying two sticks (the ones you use to play adakabεn, *xylophone*).

Even though the men were not from our villages I wanted to ask them about the children so I rose from the ground. And there, as I was about to walk into the clearing, I saw another man behind them whose hair had grown longer than a woman's, with a long beard, wearing a fugu. He looked like a man from a faraway place, but from his walk I knew it was your friend Tintin. I was shocked because I thought he was dead, but still I went forward because even ghosts, when you get close enough, are our kin. As I stepped into the clearing, I noticed that he was holding the children and an adakabεn.

Tintin, I said, where did you find these children?

And there my son ran to me with the look of someone who had done a good thing. Mensisi followed him and I held their hands.

Tintin smiled. They came to listen to my music. I was bringing them home.

Ei. What I was seeing was like a dream; this Tintin had been gone for almost four years and he was just here in our forest and I hadn't seen him. I greeted his friends and touched Tintin on the shoulder, and we embraced. Atuu, I said. Akwaaba.

Yɛn nua.

Ah, Tintin, how could the children hear you playing this small adakabɛn?

Tintin laughed. Not this one; this is a gift for the chief. The big one. I made one like the *organ* in the church.

Ei Tintin, no no no, you are lying. (I had seen the *organ* in the church and I couldn't believe him.)

Tintin shook his head. I swear my father's leg. I went to the north to learn and I came back one year ago with my friends here and we started looking for trees that would be good to make the adakabɛn with. We finished making it today; that's why the children heard me.

I looked at his face paa to see if he was joking, but he looked serious. And they can hear in the village? I asked.

He nodded.

Then let's go and show me so you can send a message to let them know I have found the children.

I am always repeating the elders' adage that even the eagle has not seen everything but, when I went to the place where Tintin had been living, where he had built the adakabɛn, sɛbi, I almost died.

He had hung the thing at about a man's height between two baobab trees, and each key was bigger than my cutlass. There were so many keys that it was hard to count them, and, even though Tintin is a tall tall man, he had to stand on a platform to play it. (Ei, this earth.) But what was wondrous was the resonators under the adakabɛn. He had used gourds the size of a woman's buttocks, suspended above the earth, swaying in the night wind, and glistening with moisture. The gourds increased in size from right to left, and, in the middle of the left side, he had cut holes and stretched goatskin over the holes so that the adakabɛn had a heavier sound. The holes got big big in the gourds until the last key, which he had connected to the hollow in the baobab tree directly, making the tree shiver with sound when he played it. I mean, there were so many strings holding the thing together that if I had seen it from a distance I would have thought a giant spider was catching things in forest.

Tintin climbed on his platform and played:

'Yɛn ahu wɔn ooh, yɛn ahu nkɔla no.'

He played it about ten times, and, even though it wasn't on a drum, I knew Oduro and the chief's okyeame would understand.

I tell you, the adakabɛn was so loud that I felt Tintin was playing my own skin, but that is how when we got back to the village everyone was waiting for us by the tweneboa tree with their fires, wondering what the sound was that had sent the message about the children.

It was in front of all the people gathered that Ananse's madness came to light. He came up to me, grabbed his child and started beating her. He slapped her face and kicked her. He knocked her head and pulled her ears. This child was four years, can you believe it? Yaa Somu went to stop him, and he knocked her to the floor, so we the men went to hold him. He hit many of us before we managed to hold him. Hmm. Something changed in the villages that night. Before then, many of the men used to beat their wives sometimes, but when we saw what Kwaku Ananse did, we finally understood why the old ones said that the brave man displays his courage and strength on the battlefield, not at home. It was not right, what we had been doing. We are given strength to protect, not to make others our slaves. So, sɛbi, it is because of Kwaku Ananse that the men stopped striking their wives in the village. Ei. That night is when I saw that what the women had said was true: the love he had for that child was not natural. I mean, he beat her many times after that, especially when she came from school (the school started by our friend from *Kenya*, who taught the children to write). But, when I think about it, there was always a boy or a man involved. It burned him. Yaa Somu saw it that night; that's why she cursed him in front of everyone, with the fires of many torches flickering in her eyes.

She picked up the child who was motionless on the ground and stood a little away from Ananse. If you beat her like that again, I will kill you, and if I'm not here, the moment she conceives, that will be the beginning of your punishment. I curse you in the name of all my ancestors. You are not a man. It is not a man who raises his hand against a woman who has sixty years. I curse you.

Indeed, it is lucky for Ananse that in the same moon Yaa Somu was killed by a speeding *truck* when she went to visit one of her older daughters in Accra for the *Independence* celebrations, for surely she would have killed him. That woman was powerful; she never failed to do what she promised.

Akosua Darko tapped their table. 'My good men. You have to leave now. You have been here since I opened.'

Kayo looked up and smiled at the woman. 'Oh, Auntie, we haven't been here long; we will soon be finished. Opanyin here is telling us a story, a very good story.' He gestured towards the hunter who was looking at Akosua with a mischievous grin on his face.

Akosua laughed. 'I have heard some of Opanyin Poku's stories before. None of them can be finished in one sitting.' She reached for the big calabash of palm wine, which they had emptied. 'Listen, others have come and eaten and gone, but you are still drinking palm wine. It is—'

'Has he told you the story of Kwaku Ananse?' Garba's speech was slurred and childlike.

Oduro put his hand on Garba's forearm. 'My friend, half of our stories in this land are about Kwaku Ananse.'

Akosua collected the hunter's calabash, which he had quickly drained, and reached for Oduro's.

'You are staying in the hut next to mine,' Oduro said. 'You won't need that tent you brought.'

Garba was still looking at Akosua, waiting for an answer to his question about Kwaku Ananse.

Akosua shook her head indulgently. 'It is now time for me to go and sleep. I will tell you tomorrow.'

Kayo drained his calabash, put it down and patted Garba on the shoulder. 'Let's go.'

Garba stood with a sudden burst of energy, gulped the rest of his palm wine, and bowed as he handed his calabash to Akosua.

*

Just before leaving Akosua Darko's place Kayo had again heard the distant strains of a xylophone. Now, he waited for Garba's breathing to settle into a steady pattern so he could go out and investigate. Two nights in a row was beyond coincidence, regardless of how much he had drunk. With his eyes still closed, he reached into the duffel bag he was using as a pillow and took out his flashlight. A few minutes later, he glanced in Garba's direction. The constable was lying on his back, his chest bare and his pistol by his right hand, exhaling softly.

Kayo crawled through the door, flinching as the mat rustled when it brushed his back. Once outside, he rose into a crouching position and crept towards the path that led to

Asare's farm. Sonokrom was in complete darkness, except for the pale light of a quarter moon, and quiet enough for a whisper to be heard. When Kayo had made it past the greening hedge at the boundary of the village he realised that he hadn't been breathing. He inhaled, flicked on his flashlight briefly to memorise the path and carried on in darkness. He planned to walk in the direction of the bamboo copse where they had burned the remains from Kofi Atta's hut, but he intended to go further north in the direction he felt he had heard the sound of the xylophone coming from.

The hunter's story was entertaining, but Kayo didn't believe it was fictional. The first night he had heard the music from the forest he had thought nothing of it, but now that the hunter had told them the story of Tintin and his giant xylophone he was convinced that could be the link between the hunter's story and recent events in Sonokrom. He wasn't quite sure what he would do if he found the xylophone, but he had a hunch that it was important. Kayo heard a movement behind him and swivelled round, bending low in case he was being attacked. He switched on the flashlight and swept the beam across the path behind him. There was nothing. The bushes swayed gently in the night air and the village looked as dark as ever. He wished he hadn't left Garba behind. There was no reason to keep this trip secret from him, especially now that Kayo was fairly sure that the constable had no deep feelings of loyalty towards Inspector Donkor.

With his head light from Akosua Darko's superb palm wine, Garba had been telling him more about how the PRCC had gained and held his influence in government.

'Mr Kayo, you know you have to solve this case by whatever means necessary?'

'No. The inspector said he wants a report, so that's what I'm working on.'

'Are you sure?' Garba leaned sideways, wagging his finger. 'Ah, you don't know this man, you don't know this man.'

'Why do you say that?'

'Mr Kayo, by now Donkor has already told the minister that the case is solved. E be so the man dey work. Why you think say the man dey progress like so? You know say all the ministers them pickins e get police dey follow them? If matter come, like accident or something, Donkor go cover am, then e go tell the minister say everything fine.' Garba laughed. 'But you then me sabi say everything no fine. What kind minister want make people sabi say im pickin cause accident?'

'I see.' Kayo nodded. 'Garba, are you happy working for the police?'

'A man with a full stomach can't complain.'

'Yeah, that's a saying, but how do you feel?'

'I enjoy some of the work – like this work with you, I'm learning how to investigate – but sometimes on the road I don't like the way everything is politics. One minute you arrest someone for drugs and the next day you go in to work and they've been released. It's not correct.'

Kayo shook his head and patted Garba on the back. They walked into their hut in silence. Oduro and Opanyin Poku had already disappeared, having left Akosua Darko's while Garba was still draining his calabash.

Kayo could smell the sweet tang that flooded the air when they burned the remains the day before. He was close to the circle of bamboo trees. From there he was in new territory. He felt like turning on his flashlight again, but decided against it. He closed his eyes and opened them slowly, trying to adjust to the moonlight. He spotted a slightly worn path and walked down it, taking long slow strides and keeping his ears pricked for any movement ahead of him. He was glad he had worn boots instead of trainers when he was leaving Accra, because he realised there could be snakes and scorpions in the undergrowth. He was always amazed to see the children in the village running around barefoot.

When he had gone over a hundred metres beyond the bamboo circle, Kayo was sure he could see a flicker of light ahead. It was about a kilometre away. He knew the light could be from another village but he was sure that those villagers would have gone to bed at the same time as the people of Sonokrom. He wished he had brought his camera. For a moment he hovered between the notions of going back to get it or carrying on, but before he could decide there was a sudden commotion to his left. A dark form came straight at him, knocked him over and bounded away. Kayo howled in pain as he hit the ground. He scrambled in the undergrowth to find his flashlight and slowly rose to his feet. As he brushed the dirt from his clothes, he heard the sound of hooves receding. A bright flame lit up the forest and he turned to see Oduro and Opanyin Poku walking towards him from the village.

'We heard you shouting,' the hunter said.

Kayo shook his head. 'It was nothing. I think an antelope knocked me over.'

Opanyin Poku crouched with the fire torch in his left hand and studied the ground near Kayo's feet. 'Duiker,' he said. 'It was probably running away from something.'

'What were you doing here?' Oduro asked.

'Just walking,' said Kayo. 'I was trying to clear the palm wine from my head before I slept and this is the only path I know.'

'You have to be careful. Some of the paths are sacred; ask before you go wandering.' Oduro walked back towards the village, leaving Kayo with the hunter.

Opanyin Poku was silent as he walked Kayo back to the

boundary of the village, but as he turned towards his hut he said, 'I can show you the paths tomorrow if you want.'

'It won't be necessary.' Kayo shook his head and looked at the ground. 'Sleep well, Opanyin.'

'Sleep well, Kwadwo.'

Once inside the hut, Kayo noticed Garba was gone. So was his gun. He walked towards the constable's mat as if expecting him to appear.

'Mr Kayo.'

Kayo jumped at the voice behind him. It was Garba, with a cloth tied around his waist and his pistol snug behind the knot. His chest was still bare.

'Garba! Where were you?'

'I followed you, sah.'

'You followed me? Did you see the old men?'

'Yes.' Garba took the pistol out and laid it back on the floor as he settled down to sleep. 'What were you looking for?'

Kayo chuckled. 'You'll laugh.'

'I swear on my grandmother's leg, I won't laugh.'

'I was looking for the musician, Tintin.'

'Thank God my grandmother is already dead,' Garba laughed. 'You drank too much, sah.'

'And the xylophone.'

'Mr Kayo, it's just a story.'

Kayo stretched to his full height on the mat and exhaled. 'I know, Garba.' He closed his eyes, straining to hear the echo of a xylophone as he drifted to sleep.

fida

KAYO EXTENDED HIS TOES AND SQUINTED AT THE SUNLIGHT
that had come to settle on him through the window-hole of
the hut. His first impression was that everything was absolutely
quiet, but after a few minutes he became aware of the sounds
of chickens clucking, and, in the distance, the cooing of pigeons.
He put his hand to his face where the mat's pattern had
imprinted itself on his skin and closed his eyes again. He'd
slept longer than he had intended; Garba's mat on the other
side of the hut was bare, and the door covering had been
raised.

After turning on to his front to do fifty quick push-ups,
Kayo rolled his mat, propped it against the wall of the hut and
headed outside without bothering to put on a shirt.

There was no one immediately outside the hut, but, twenty
metres to his left, on the felled palm by the tweneboa tree, the
hunter was sitting beside an elderly woman, holding a radio
to his ear. He waved when he saw Kayo. The Range Rover
looked out of place, lodged in front of the tree, with its high
antennae and dark blue gleam. Kayo waved back at the hunter.
He wanted to ask some of the villagers about Kofi Atta today
so he could begin to piece together a coherent hypothesis of
what had happened in Kofi Atta's hut. Even if he didn't come
up with what Inspector Donkor wanted, Kayo needed to know
the truth for himself.

What he had so far was nothing. All he could say for certain was what didn't happen; with these baked mud floors he couldn't even pick up footprints accurately. Indeed, even if they had found an entire body which could be identified, no criminal case could be made with the information he had.

Kayo shook his head. It was like his grandfather's death all over again; without a story, without witnesses, without a confession, he might as well be a ten-year-old with wild suspicions. The difference was this time he didn't suspect anyone. He had the distinct feeling that the villagers he had met knew more than they were telling, in fact he was certain Oduro and the hunter knew more than they were telling, but none of them had that air of false composure that guilt lends to its carriers.

'Mr Kayo, Mr Kayo!'

Kayo looked up to see Garba stopping to greet Opanyin Poku then jogging towards Kayo as though he had just seen his only friend after a long separation. Garba was also shirtless and his large hands were laden with ripe mangoes.

When Garba reached Kayo, he held out three mangoes. 'Morning, morning Mr Kayo. You slept well?' There was a mischievous smile playing at the edge of his lips.

Kayo took the fruit and nodded. He wiped one of the mangoes on his trousers and bit into the flesh. It was sweet.

'Chale, the people for this village no dey fear police ooh. I go interview the people for that side.' He raised his right arm towards the huts on the other side of the tweneboa tree. 'So so they dey laugh laugh with me.'

Kayo resisted the urge to ask Garba what he expected when he went to work barechested. He smiled instead. Garba was probably right. The police probably never came here; they lived in small autonomous groups and, if he was to be cynical, there was nobody to harass for bribes. It was refreshing to find a corner of the country where the fearsome reputation of the police had no effect. Kayo spat out a piece of tough mango peel. 'Wey people you go interview?'

Garba pointed to the far east of the village, where three huts were huddled around Akosua Darko's place. 'The three for there. One be Akosua Darko.' Garba smiled as he said this. 'Then one be some driver im house. The driver no dey but the wife and pickins dey. One the pickins dey sick; she say she go come see you.'

'She go come see me? Why?' Kayo tossed the now bald mango seed into a row of bushes by the hut.

'Abi you be doctor.'

Kayo looked to the sky in frustration. 'Oh, Garba! I no be doctor true true ooh.'

'No, Mr Kayo, e no be me tell am so. E be the old man, Oduro, wey e tell am so.'

'Fine,' Kayo exhaled heavily. 'So the people wey you go interview, what they tell you?'

Garba took a notebook from his pocket, and, for a moment, Kayo felt a wave of anger as he remembered the night Garba and Sergeant Ofosu had arrested him. The feeling passed quickly as Kayo reasoned that Garba was as much a victim of the power structure as he was. Besides, a man who kept a notebook was a man who respected logic and order and Kayo liked that. He scratched his chin and smiled.

Garba ran a pen down his page. 'Akosua Darko then im daughter then son, they say they no see anything. They no see Kofi Atta since three months. The driver im there, the pickin wey e dey sick, e say e see Kofi Atta like one month now, wey e say the man dey look young.'

'Young?'

'Yeah, like say e dye im hair. The grey hairs all comot.'

'I see. Who again you talk plus?'

'Ei, the last hut, they play law plus me. They say I no get warrant. E be them give me the mangoes. I think say the man be farmer; they get plenty food for there.'

Kayo weighed the information he had been given. It didn't tell him much, but the sick girl's last sighting of Kofi Atta tallied with the hunter's sighting of about a month ago. That left a gap of just over three weeks which he had to fill in somehow. Kayo looked up towards the village centre where the children had begun to gather. One of the little boys tapped the base of the Range Rover's longest antenna, then ran off as Opanyin Poku shooed him.

'Garba,' Kayo turned to face the constable. 'Could you radio Mensah and ask him if he has collected my results from our friend?'

'No problem.'

'If he has, please ask him to fax them to Koforidua HQ for you to pick up.' Kayo snatched Garba's notebook and opened it.

'Oh, Mr Kayo.' Garba looked embarrassed.

It was a new notebook, not the one he had in Accra, and the latest page was headed *Sonokrom Investigations Day Three*. Garba had listed the huts that he had visited by number: *Hut One, Hut Two, Hut Three*. Kayo smiled and handed the notebook back to Garba. 'Thank you for your interview work. I think I'll let you do the rest while I try to model the incident scene on my laptop.'

'Sure, Mr Kayo.' Garba walked briskly towards the Range Rover.

'Garba, wait.' Kayo raised his arm. 'I'll come with you. The laptop is still in the car.'

As Kayo drew close to Garba he whispered. 'Why are the children not in school? It's Friday.'

'Oh, have you forgotten? It's July; they are on long vacation.'

'Ah, true.' Kayo stopped at the tweneboa tree and greeted Opanyin Poku.

The hunter nodded. 'I greet you, Kwadwo. I'm listening to Sunrise FM, Koforidua.' His face was animated.

Kayo put his hands behind his back. 'Is this your wife? Ma, I greet you.'

The hunter put his arm around the woman sitting beside him as though he had just remembered that she was there. 'Ehh, this is Mama Aku, my wife.'

The woman smiled and spoke to Kayo in Ga. 'Welcome. I hear you are from Accra. We receive you with open arms.' She put a hand on the hunter's short-cropped head and continued. 'And if my husband here starts telling you stories, don't pay him any mind; he's full of them.'

'Yes Ma.' Kayo left the hunter and his wife to rejoin Garba by the Range Rover. He grabbed his laptop bag and extra batteries and headed towards the hut while Garba radioed Accra.

Kayo had barely covered half the distance between the tweneboa tree and the hut when a fury of footsteps reached him, raising dust in their wake. He stopped to avoid collision, and was surprised to see it was Kusi, his arm still bound in the cloth that Oduro had provided, but running as though he had full use of both arms.

The boy stopped and squinted up at Kayo. 'Uncle Kwadwo, my mother said I should come and say thank you.'

'Ehh? Tell your mother I said thank you for telling you to say thank you. How is the arm?'

Kusi raised his broken arm as though he were trying to give it to Kayo. 'It's fine.' He brought the arm back down and pointed at the laptop bag with his left hand. 'What is that?'

Kayo smiled. 'It's my computer. I have to do some work with it.'

'My mother said you are looking for Egya Kofi Atta.'

'That's true. Have you seen him?'

'No.' Kusi looked at his dusty feet. 'But I saw a boy going into his hut. He wasn't from this village.'

Kayo squatted in front of Kusi. 'Ehh? Do you remember how long ago?'

'About two weeks.'

'Tintin!'

Both Kayo and Kusi swivelled around to see who had called.

There was nobody visible, but Kayo saw a movement in a milkbush close to a hut to his left and pointed at it.

As if on cue a group of five kids emerged and ran off giggling.

Kusi took off after them screaming. 'Heh, Kakra, Panyin, Oforiwaa . . .'

And together they disappeared into a cluster of trees.

Kayo spent the morning sitting on a mat in the middle of the hut that Oduro had said the chief had assigned them, referring to his green notebook and creating a virtual replica of the interior and exterior of Kofi Atta's hut. Paying great attention to scale, he positioned the window-hole and the doorway and placed the furniture according to the measurements DC Mensah had taken.

He was still puzzled by the whole case, yet he knew Inspector Donkor expected results very fast. The man was probably trying to beat some promotion deadline. Kayo chuckled to himself, then stopped. From the inspector's erratic behaviour when Kayo went to see him in Accra, it occurred to Kayo that his own life could be in danger if he didn't deliver a 'CSI-style' report at the end of the week. Kayo had never seen a report delivered in CSI, in all the time he had been watching it, but who was he to contradict the inspector? Still, his mind was plagued by what Kusi, had told him. What would a young boy be doing going into Kofi Atta's hut?

A few hours after midday, Garba popped in to report that he was going to Koforidua to pick up the results that Kayo had asked for.

'Anything new from the interviews?' Kayo pulled his digital camera out of his canvas duffel bag.

'Nothing Mr Kayo. Nobody has seen him since about a month now.' Garba scratched his chin; there was some overnight growth, which made it sound like a distant saw. 'But the palm-wine man, Owusu, said he heard a pot breaking. I think maybe it's the same pot you asked me to number that day.'

'When did he say he heard it?'

'Late night or early morning before the minister's girl came.'

'Did he do anything?'

'Nothing. He said pots break all the time, especially near him, because of the palm wine. He thought it was one of his own pots but he didn't get up; he said "bed sweet".' Garba laughed, and then added with a leer, 'His wife is very fine. Fine woman.'

Kayo shook his head. 'You see? I ask you to go interview, and you go around looking at women.'

Something like a cackle escaped Garba's throat. 'Not so, Mr Kayo, not so.'

'It's OK.' Kayo held up his hand. 'You just go to Koforidua and bring my results.'

'Yes sah ooh.' Garba stood to attention and did an about-turn.

Kayo clicked his fingers. 'Leave your notebook.'

Garba turned back to Kayo, handed him the notebook, and marched out of the hut chuckling.

Kayo plugged his camera into his laptop and downloaded the pictures he had taken from the hut. After scaling and editing the images, he superimposed them within the 3D digital diagram of Kofi Atta's hut that he had created. When he had finished, he took out his notebook and drew the floor plan of the scene in pencil so that he could think it through. In spite of his familiarity with advanced modelling programs, he found that he could never think as effectively when working from the screen. He needed his notebook so that he could make notes, draw arrows; he needed to feel the scene beneath his fingers.

What Garba had told him almost eliminated the possibility that the pot was broken by the minister's girlfriend and her driver when they entered the hut, so it had to figure in his hypothesis.

Kayo flicked through his notebook absent-mindedly, stopping every couple of pages to look at points that he had marked with asterisks. From the testimony of the minister's girlfriend, she had been led to the remains by a foul smell after she stopped to follow a blue-headed bird; after that the account was largely incoherent, but she insisted she saw the same thing the police saw. However, Kayo seemed to remember a section in her transcript where she said she saw the thing move. He had dismissed it earlier, but now he wanted to be sure. They had encountered too many unexplained phenomena to dismiss any; maybe together they would make sense. He marked his page in the notebook with the blue feather he had kept from Kofi Atta's hut, reached for the folder that Inspector Donkor had given him, removed the transcript and scanned it.

There it was:

What was in the hut?

I don't know. It was evil.

Was it similar to anything you had seen before?

No, it was evil.

Can you describe it?

It was evil, it was red and it moved.

121

Madam, are you sure it moved? You said earlier that it was dark.

I swear it moved. It was evil.

Kayo scanned the section over and over. Logically, he couldn't accept that the remains he had come to find could have moved, but based on the hunter's assessment of the maggots, it was a possibility. The maggots seemed to suggest that whatever it was they found only died on the day that the minister's girlfriend saw it, or, at worst, the day before.

Kayo wrote in bullet points: *Living thing, human according to laboratory results, foul-smelling, red, villagers immune to smell according to my observation and police report . . .* He stopped and went back to the fourth bullet point, *red*, and frowned. The flies. The police report prepared by Sergeant Ofosu asserted that the remains were black and appeared to be moving. Only on approaching the remains did the flies disperse to reveal that the remains were red. If the minister's girlfriend, who ran away from the *evil* as soon as she saw it, said it was red, then it was likely that there were no flies at that time. Kayo tapped his pen against his notebook, bobbing his head to the beat.

So he had a broken pot – which may or may not have been broken the night before the remains were discovered; discrete patches of urine, some of which had an indistinct trapezoid shape; no blood splatter; maggots that dated the period of decay at the time of his arrival at between three and four days; the sighting of a boy entering Kofi Atta's hut approximately two weeks before the discovery of the remains – to be confirmed; sightings of Kofi Atta – who remained missing – outside, about a month before the discovery of the remains. Kofi Atta was described as a widowed man, whose only daughter had left him, and had no real friends – a loner. The kind of profile that at West Midlands Police, he might have attributed to a sociopath, which Kofi Atta probably was. But where was he?

Kayo was aware that he had nothing. Of course there were the things that he didn't dare begin to tackle as yet, such as the spectacle at Kofi Atta's hut after they had burned the remains. All those birds! Still, he was certain that key people in the village were holding information back from him. Everything was too serene considering that a man was missing from a village with just twelve families. Kayo knew that if he was to make a breakthrough, it would have to be today, when Garba brought the DNA results. Kayo had taken his samples with no logic whatsoever; it wasn't even based on hunches, simply opportunity: a swab of sweat from Opanyin Poku when he put his arm around his shoulders, saliva from Akosua Darko when he asked her to taste his wine, sweat from Oduro's hand-shake, and a sample from the remains. It was tenuous, but in a community as small as this one, someone was bound to be related to the remains. It was his best chance of unsettling the balance, causing enough discomfort to make someone talk.

By the time Garba returned from Koforidua, Kayo had worked himself close to despair by going over the information they had gathered again and again. He had worked non-stop, except for one interruption from the truck driver's daughter, who wasn't so much sick as expecting. He had simply asked her a few questions since he didn't really have any supplies. She readily admitted that she was urinating more frequently than usual, but laughed when Kayo asked her if her breasts were tender.

'Are you trying to seduce me?' There was a knowing twinkle in her eye.

Kayo smiled, 'No, I'm trying to find out if someone else has recently.'

She cast her eyes to the floor, then raised them slowly. 'Why?'

'Maybe, sɛbi, he is the reason you are ill.'

'Oh, really?' Her eyes widened as she realised what Kayo was trying to say, then she smiled. 'Oh!' She turned and headed for the door, looking back to wave. 'I thank you,' she giggled. Then she was gone.

Hours later Kayo still had more questions in his notepad than answers. Key among the questions was the pattern of the urine spill. He realised that on a mud floor there was bound to be some error due to spreading, but the shape of the smaller patches definitely tapered. The problem was that they tapered in the wrong direction for a moving spillage; the wider side of the spill's trapezium was supposed to be oriented towards the largest patch, but it was the opposite.

'Ayekoo.'

Kayo looked up from his notebook, mildly irritated with himself. It was a purple dusk outside. Garba stood in the doorway with Oduro, smiling.

'We said ayekoo.' Garba walked towards Kayo, holding out an envelope.

Kayo didn't feel like he had done much work, but he responded, 'Yaa ye.' It was standard call and response; he wasn't even sure if there was an option to suggest that you hadn't been working hard. Once someone said 'ayekoo' it was as though they had judged you and decided that you had worked hard. It was binding and final.

'We have to go and eat,' said Oduro from the doorway. 'Your friend here says you have only eaten three mangoes today.'

Kayo took the envelope from Garba and put it in his back pocket. He grabbed a blue T-shirt from his duffel bag, put it on and walked towards the medicine man with Garba. 'My friend also says that you have been telling people that I'm a doctor.'

Oduro laughed as he turned to lead them towards Akosua Darko's place. 'But it's true. You have helped me paa.'

'Ehh? The girl who you sent to me this afternoon is pregnant.' Kayo took the envelope from his pocket and peered at its contents. He stopped suddenly, took out a sheet and frowned.

'What is wrong?' Oduro asked.

'Nothing.' Kayo smiled. 'I didn't tell her that she was pregnant, so maybe you can speak to her mother.'

Oduro quickened his steps. 'I'll do it. Let's hurry to Akosua Darko's; Opanyin Poku is waiting.'

Akosua Darko's place was bustling. There were people packed on all the tables, and many standing, drinking palm wine. There were certainly more people than were usually in the entire Sonokrom.

Kayo placed a palm on Oduro's back, just below his leopard-claw chain, making the medicine man turn around. 'Where are all these people from?'

Oduro laughed. 'This place is famous for the softest fufu in the Eastern Region, so when Friday comes, we get people from the sixteen villages, plus contractors in the area – even people from Koforidua. Kwaku Wusu's palm wine is also very popular.'

Pushing through the throng after Oduro and Garba, Kayo spotted Opanyin Poku with his wife sitting at a table next to the one they had been sitting at the day before. Eager to make it to a seat, Kayo bumped into a woman who almost spilled the calabash of palm wine she was holding. She turned around and Kayo almost stumbled when he saw that it was Akosua's daughter, Esi. She had a white and blue wax print cloth wrapped around her breasts and her skin had a light covering of talcum powder, with what appeared to be two circular tattoos above the line of the cloth.

Esi smiled when she saw him and put a hand on his shoulder to steady herself. 'Oh, Kwadwo, how are you?'

'I'm fine.' Kayo avoided the twinkle in her eye and stared at her forehead. 'How do you know my name?'

'I overheard it yesterday.' She nodded and walked off towards the rear of the hut.

Kayo continued to the table and sat down between Oduro and Garba after shaking hands with the hunter and his wife.

'They are bringing your palm wine.' Opanyin Poku pointed at the empty spots in front of Kayo, Garba and Oduro.

'Good,' said Garba. 'Can we order food too? I'm hungry.'

'Do you want fufu or palaver sauce?' asked Mama Aku.

'I'll have the palaver sauce,' said Kayo. 'With apem, if they have it.'

'As for me, I'll have the fufu again.' Garba rubbed his stomach.

Opanyin Poku made a series of hand signals to a young man at the rear doorway and then turned back to the table. 'So, have you prepared yourselves for the rest of my story?'

Garba shook his head. 'Can we drink first? It's better with the drink.' He turned to Oduro. 'Do you have your thing?'

Oduro untied the knot in his waistcloth and extracted a vial. 'This one is different from what we had yesterday; it's from the root of bonsamdua.'

Kayo watched Garba discussing the merits and demerits of using different herbs for strengthening palm wine, and thought of how similar he was to Nii Nortey in some respects. The same infantile enthusiasm for food and drink, and an easy familiarity with strangers and strangeness. Kayo himself had become a more questioning sort with age and immersion into science, a bent that had curbed his inborn enthusiasm. As he scanned the heaving interior of Akosua Darko's place, he wondered if, to fully experience humanity, you had to be continually open to novelty, the strange. After all, truth was something that shifted depending on the range of your exposure. Ghanaians were reputed to be some of the friendliest people on earth – perhaps because of this very openness – but he also knew that they judged people, and kept people at bay; they weren't unreservedly open, that was a myth. That was why, in spite of Sonokrom's welcoming attitude to him, he had to remain cautious. He liked the hunter, and Oduro, and this dark place with its fine drink, but he had to remain on guard. He placed a palm on the dark wood of the table and looked around.

The room was alive with flesh. A surfeit of work sweat that prodded at the nostrils and the humidity tingled on skin. There was also the green smell of the forest and faint undertones of talcum and local perfumes, perhaps like the one Garba had told him about, bediwunua. Kayo suppressed a chuckle as his eyes swept the room. He had never seen so much bare flesh in his life – not even on the shore, when the fishermen were pulling nets in. There had to be close to a hundred people in the place. Kayo could easily tell who the contractors and visitors from Koforidua were, because, like him, they were wearing shirts. The rest of the customers wore a kaleidoscope of tie and dye, wax print or batik, tied around their waists or breasts. Some of the men had their cloths wrapped around their chests, crossed over at the front and tied behind their necks to create a sort of backless one-piece. However, as soon as they got a seat and were served, they undid the knots behind their necks, dropped the cloths to their waists and faced the food full on.

Kayo brought his attention back to the table. The hunter was whispering something into his wife's ear, and Kayo studied him in the light of the tests that Joseph had done for him, the results that DC Mensah had faxed to Koforidua, the Eastern Region HQ, that were lodged in his pocket right then. Kayo found it difficult to believe the results but he knew that Joseph would have double-checked. In all the time he had worked with him Kayo had never known Joseph to make a mistake. Of course, Mr Acquah, in his carpeted office, probably had no idea how much of an asset Joseph was to his company. With Kayo gone, his laboratory would fall into chaos if Joseph were to leave too.

Esi arrived with three calabashes, placed them in front of Garba, Oduro and Kayo, and filled them with palm wine, a shy smile hovering on her face.

As she headed back to the kitchen area in the rear, Mama Aku said, 'Kwadwo, I think she likes you.'

Kayo shook his head. 'She's just shy.' He tasted his palm wine. 'Do you know what she has on her shoulder? Those marks?'

'Ah,' the hunter leaned forward. 'It's from a fruit, from a bush called mmofra forowa. They cut the fruit in half to get the pattern, then they dip it in dye and use it on the skin.'

'It's beautiful.' Kayo signalled to Oduro to add some of his bonsamdua extract to his palm wine.

'Of course it's beautiful.' The hunter pointed at Kayo and laughed. 'It's even more beautiful when it is on beautiful skin.'

Oduro, Garba and Mama Aku joined in the hunter's laughter.

Then Oduro held up his hand and said: 'Yes, the sky is beautiful, but if a vine is to see the sky it needs a tree to climb.'

This time Kayo joined in the laughter. He had always thought of proverbs as things his parents said to befuddle him, but now he could see the life in them.

The hunter also held up his hand. 'So, I am continuing my story.' He turned to his wife. 'Mama Aku, you know the story so I will just continue: Yaa Somu has cursed Kwaku Ananse for the way he beat his child, but on Independence Day, Yaa Somu died and everything in the child's life changed.'

*

When Yaa Somu died, there was a big funeral in K Krom. Big big funeral paa. We had people from all the sixteen villages and beyond because, sɛbi, Yaa Somu was someone who was respected paa. When she was younger and sold tomatoes, she would always save some of her produce for those who didn't have much. Her older daughters followed her into trading, but they married and went to Accra to trade in the big market there. Oh, we all cried, the whole village, even Kwaku Ananse, because, sɛbi, in spite of his foolishness, he knew that she had cared for him.

The child, Mensisi, was also tied up with sadness. Indeed she didn't eat properly for many days after Yaa Somu died and she didn't. talk; she just stared, stared all day. I think that Mensisi's silence made her father feel guilty, because he didn't beat her for many moons – or maybe it was because he was afraid of the curse. He cared for the child as before, and with Yaa Somu gone, he came back from his farm earlier to cook for her. Sometimes, during the day, I would care for the child because I came back from forest early, otherwise he left her with one of the other families. I have to say that we tried to convince Kwaku Ananse to marry again, because he was still young, not even twenty-eight. I mean, we thought if he was with a woman he would let the child be, but he said he didn't want any more children.

So, after Yaa Somu died, we can say that things changed, but many things remained the same. I mean, as soon as the girl started to go to the *Kenyan* man to learn to read and write, the beatings started again. In the beginning we didn't know; he used to pull her ears and pinch her when she returned from studying.

He would say: So you think you will be wiser than your father? Did they teach you how not to feel pain?

Then he would pull her ears and drag her to her stool to eat. You can fill your head with stupidity all day, but remember I am the one that fills your stomach.

And then (this is the madness) he would sit with her and say *ABC* with her, and tell her stories about her mother as if he had done nothing unusual.

This is why we didn't know, because the child didn't know what to think so she didn't tell anyone. She never told, never. But Mensisi had a good brain, she was learning quickly, and our friend from *Kenya* loved teaching her, so he started taking her to his home with the other kids (remember, the village was small, so there were only six children learning to read and write) for his wife to feed them before he sent them home. Our *Kenyan* friend had a farm so there was always plenty of food in his home, and his wife, a woman from the village, could cook paa. So, because of the food that the children were given, Mensisi went home full and often struggled to eat.

One day, when she got home she couldn't eat at all and she told Kwaku Ananse that she had eaten already. And there, sɛbi, the real trouble began. He beat her until she couldn't cry anymore; she just whimpered like a dog. He left her on the floor and ate the food he had cooked for her, then he walked her to the stream to go and bathe.

In the light of the next morning we all saw the swellings on her face so, we the men, we sat together and decided that Oduro, the medicine man, should go and talk to Kwaku Ananse.

Ei! If I tell you that Kwaku Ananse told Oduro to leave his home, there you will understand why the wise ones said that when one starts on the path to evil good counsel sounds like a joke. He told Oduro to leave him alone; the same Oduro who he had asked to plead with the ancestors so that his farm would be successful – he had forgotten.

Still, Oduro told Kwaku Ananse that Yaa Somu's curse was not an idle curse, so he should mend his ways, because, sɛbi, when the time comes, nobody would be able to help him if he had refused to placate the ancestors. It was good counsel, but Kwaku Ananse's madness had come to stay.

So, this is how the child, Mensisi, grew up. He would beat her, then he would be kind to her, and, whenever anyone asked where her bruises were from, she would lie for him, because she didn't want trouble for him. Sometimes we heard him beating her, or shouting at her, telling her that she had killed his wife, she was anyɛn like her grandmother, Yaa Somu. There wasn't much we could do. I mean, sɛbi, she was his daughter and the ancestors must lead the way, but there were times when we called on them to ask for things we didn't need, just so that he would stop beating her.

When Mensisi reached the age of twelve, our friend from *Kenya* went to Kwaku Ananse to tell him that his child had a good mind, that she knew things, so it would be good for her to do *exams* and go to *secondary school*. Kwaku Ananse didn't even give the matter the appropriate time to think about it; he started shaking his head before the man had even finished talking.

My daughter is not going anywhere. I have work for her here.

Please, just think about it.

I said no. Are you stupid? Are you listening to me?

It is true that Kwaku Ananse had become very unpleasant over the years. He no longer had any real friends in the village. He wouldn't even let the child's aunts from Accra take her to see her cousins. When people took care of the child it was because of the memory of Yaa Somu or the child's mother, or because they liked the child, who by now was even more gracious and beautiful than her mother had ever been. Maybe, sɛbi, having no friends, Kwaku Ananse wanted to keep the only person he loved close by.

As for me, I don't know, even now I don't know, but that is how Mensisi's education ended. But the girl herself was stubborn. (Yesterday I told you that she knew what she wanted from when she was little.) She decided that if she wouldn't get to go to school she would trade, like her grandmother. By Onyame's generosity, Yaa Somu's land, where she planted her tomatoes, had not been taken by anyone (I think the chief in his wisdom kept it so), so Mensisi got my sons to help her clear it and she started planting tomatoes. Kwaku Ananse was not happy, but, sɛbi, apart from beating her he couldn't do anything to her, and she was no longer afraid of the weight of his arm.

So, this is how Mensisi became a tomato trader like her grandmother. Oh no (I've made a mistake) I mean when she started she planted the tomatoes and sold her harvest to other traders. She carried on like that for four years before she started selling tomatoes herself by the basket. She used to sit by the road with some other traders, some sold cassava, some sold onions, some sold plantain, and when these businessmen came past on their way home from treks, they would stop and buy something. Mensisi still sold some of her crop to other traders, but she made more money by the road.

Those who only follow what can be seen will say the child chose to go to the road, but there are those who will know that the road came for her, for is it not the same road that took her grandmother out of the village? Ehh, Yaa Somu was killed on the road on the day that this land of ours celebrated freedom. So it was, that we thought that the road had brought freedom to Mensisi when the new *government* sent *surveyors* to come and find a good place to build a new road.

You see, the men who came, they were all young. They had been trained in schools on the other side of the sea (like our Kwadwo here) to use tools to look at the land differently. In our day, all we would have done is walk the land until we found a place that was right for what we wanted, but these men, they had these things on legs that they looked through – and though they travelled the land too, they didn't cover as much distance as we would have. There were many of them, but one of them, hmm . . . let us say that his work always brought him to where Mensisi was selling her tomatoes. He would stop and talk to her and sometimes explain the job he was doing. As I have said, Mensisi was not a fool; when he showed her his job, she asked him questions and even made him change his mind. Truly, he was there so much that all the other traders started calling him Mensisi's husband. Every time he was going back to Accra, he would buy a basket of each of the produce that they had at the roadside and load it at the back of one of those *trucks* they used. It was not long before news of this boy, this man (he was called James), reached Kwaku Ananse, and, I believe I don't have to tell you what descended there.

It was the worst beating we had seen and it was right in the village centre. By this time Mensisi was big enough to defend herself but, surprisingly, she just stood there and let him beat her. I had never seen anything like it; it was as though she was leaving someone else, something else, to fight for her. We could see it in her eyes. There was no fear, no pain. She just looked at him as he hit her. Even when we, the men, were called from our homes to go and hold Kwaku Ananse, she didn't move from the spot from where he attacked her. It was right beside a fan palm tree, and she stood there, quiet quiet until rain began to fall.

At first the rain didn't fall hard; she stood in the water until she was completely soaked and then walked away. In no time after that, the fan palm was struck by lightning and fell. The rain fell until morning came. I mean, many of us didn't go to our work; we stayed home and played Oware with our loved ones. Tintin even had that game called *Ludo* from his travels. As I am saying this you are looking at me, but this was '71. And in '71 there was a drought in this land. The rivers were low and harvests were not good. That's why the James man used to buy so much produce to take to Accra. So we were all in our homes when we heard Kwaku Ananse shouting his daughter's name.

'Mensisi, Mensisi . . . Mensisi, where are you? Mensisi.'

We all went to our doors to look at what was happening, and there we saw Kwaku Ananse sitting on this fan palm that I told you was struck by lightning, crying. Crying paa – the way sheep do when they give birth. And then he would shout Mensisi's name.

We were standing there looking when Mensisi emerged from her grandmother's hut and asked her father, What? What do you want?

Kwaku Ananse looked at Mensisi in the doorway of Yaa Somu's hut and he couldn't speak. I think he saw then, in that doorway, the incarnation of Yaa Somu's curse. We also saw it. I mean, Mensisi was bruised and limping but we could see that he couldn't hurt her anymore. And those of us who have eyes, we also saw the tree. The fan palm that Kwaku Ananse was sitting on. Can you believe that this thing, the tree, was felled from its base? By lightning? My brothers, this earth is full of wonders. This was no ordinary tree fallen, it was a sign, and nobody moved that tree from where it fell. The leaves died and were consumed by the earth, but the wood itself, it is still there.

When the sun came, the young man James came to the village to look for Mensisi. I think, wherever he went, when he got there he realised he had left something behind. So he came back. He came back well prepared, with an elderly uncle, a bottle of *schnapps* and some cloth. It was in his mind to ask for Mensisi's hand, but when he came and saw her the way she was, he decided to take her to a *hospital*. Since he was staying in Kumasi at the time, he took her to the *hospital* there. He left the *schnapps* and the cloth with me (Kwaku Ananse had gone to check on his cocoa) and said he would be back to perform the rites and ask for her hand. Hmm. We didn't see him again for many moons.

One menada, me and my wife were sitting on the palm wood that fell during the storm. We were talking about our chief; he had just bought one of these new Akasanoma radios and it was the only radio in the sixteen villages. My wife had heard it the day before when she had gone to take him his share of my hunting meat (I usually give him the two hind legs – it's what he likes) and she was telling me about the wonders it could do. I mean, we thought Tintin's adakabɛn was a wonder, but the Akasanoma was small, just a small box, and it could play music from Accra, Tamale, Takoradi, Kumasi and you could hear men and women speaking in it. After my wife told me about it, I went to see it myself and I made my mind that one day, I would get my own Akasanoma and listen with my wife.

We were sitting there on the wood when some car came, one of these *old-type* cars, I think *Peugeot*, and who should come out but this man James and Mensisi. Ei! This was big news, because Mensisi had been gone a long time, and Kwaku

Ananse had not been happy. He had even gone to the chief to put his grievances before him, but the chief said even though it was customary for the appropriate rites to be performed, Mensisi, sɛbi, was a grown woman, and besides, they didn't know where she was to summon her.

Mensisi was looking well, but, sɛbi, herself had turned. As soon as my wife saw her, she said, as for this one, she will give birth in less than five moons. Hmm. It seems that when Mensisi went to the hospital, the doctor said that somebody had been beating her. When they asked her, she shook her head, and you know in this land we don't like matter so they left her affairs to her. The only thing was Mensisi didn't want to come back to the village immediately. She had seen one of James' books and started reading and she wanted to know what happened before she came back.

The problem was that when she stayed in James' house in Kumasi, they couldn't control themselves, so they started to live as husband and wife. (You know, sɛbi, the thing is sweet, so you understand.) Also, there were many books so Mensisi was always reading.

Let me say right here that Kwaku Ananse had good reason to be upset. Mensisi had been gone for two years and she hadn't even sent a message back home to say, sɛbi, I am not dead. If Kwaku Ananse was upset, everyone would understand, but his actions surprised us all.

Just as my wife and I greeted Mensisi and James, Kwaku Ananse, who had heard the car, emerged from his home (everyone who was in their home came out) and saw them. Kwaku Ananse had been sick for three or more moons. He coughed a lot and we hadn't seen him much, but when he saw his daughter, he strengthened himself.

He ran towards them. Mensisi, he shouted, Mensisi, is that you? Mensisi, my child, is that you?

It is I, Paapa, it is I.

And there Kwaku Ananse embraced her and greeted James. When he stood back a little, he saw that Mensisi's self had turned, so he said, 'Are you bringing me a grandchild?'

And she said, Yes, Paapa.

This was a union that the whole village witnessed. Then Kwaku Ananse had a talk with James and they agreed that Mensisi would stay with Kwaku Ananse for one nawotwe until James came with his people to perform the marriage rites. After that, she would stay another nawotwe before James could come and take her to live with him. So Mensisi came to be among us again and it was something beautiful to witness. Her father took care of her the way he had taken care of his own wife. He cooked for her, and spent a lot of time talking to her about Kumasi and the wonders there. He even wanted to know if she had met the Asantehene, who is the chief above all our chiefs here.

The next menada, James came with his elderly uncle again and I produced the *schnapps* and cloth for the rites. James' uncle explained that the women of James' family had gone to consult with the women of Mensisi's family in Accra and everything had been settled there. All that was required now was the father's blessing.

Kwaku Ananse stood and thanked James and his uncle for coming, then he expressed his grievances about the way his daughter had been taken from him. (You see how he forgot the reason why?) But, he said, for a man, all that there is, is to see your children happy, and when I look at my child, Mensisi, I can see that she has happiness paa.

And there, he nodded at me and I opened the drink, poured some for the ancestors and drank one *tot*. After that, all the senior men drank and it was settled.

Hmm. If you have watched birds, you will see that at the

time it is just about to rain, they all go quiet quiet, but apart from that, birds are only quiet when they sleep. But those of us who were here in '73, we heard the birds in the village go quiet when there was no rain. It was the moment Kwaku Ananse's hand fell on Mensisi. Oh, just look, look at how everything had gone beautifully and we were all happy for Mensisi. I mean, we thought Kwaku Ananse's madness had gone, but we were there and we heard Mensisi scream. It was daytime and all the men had gone to their work but I was in my home, lying with my wife. When we heard the sound, she lifted her leg off me and I got up to look for my cloth.

Because I thought I was the only man in the village who was not out working, and I knew Kwaku Ananse was very strong, I took my long gun. When I got to Kwaku Ananse's home, Oduro was already there trying to stop him from kicking Mensisi, who was lying on the floor. As soon as I saw the way blood was coming from Mensisi, I raised my long gun to Kwaku Ananse's chest and said, If you don't stop acting like a beast, I will kill you like a beast. And there he stood still and allowed Oduro to take Mensisi away to treat her bruises. Unfortunately, the blood didn't stop and that night I saw Mensisi going to forest. I followed her to make sure that she would be safe and, will you believe she went to the same place she went to when she walked into forest as a child? She went to Tintin's adakabɛn. Tintin was now back in the village, but there was still the small home he built near the adakabɛn.

Mensisi climbed onto the platform and passed her hands over the keys of the adakabɛn, then she got down and sat on the ground beside Tintin's home and started crying. Watching her, you could tell that all the love she had inside her was in her tears. She cried and cried, and then she held her belly. It was as if she knew what was going to happen. She took the axe Tintin had used to cut the trees for his adakabɛn. My mind told me that she was going to hurt herself, so I prepared myself to stop her.

She went into the hole under the baobab and struck the ground with the axe. (All this time she was crying.) When she had dug a hole, she lifted her cloth (I turned my eyes) and squatted over it. The baobab shivered as she screamed, and then, with her bloodied hand, she tore her cloth, put a piece over the dead child, and covered the hole. She came out and walked back to the village.

Can you believe that this was just two days before James was to come back and take Mensisi with him? It was so sad. Ah, when James came, it took more than six men to stop him from killing Kwaku Ananse. He said he was going to get Kwaku Ananse arrested, but Mensisi begged him to leave her father alone. What was more shocking (it was Oduro who pointed it out later) was that Kwaku Ananse's coughing, his illness, went.

It was there that Oduro first saw that maybe Yaa Somu's curse was working, so he went to speak with Kwaku Ananse. Oduro told Kwaku Ananse that if he was to have any chance of saving him from the curse, Kwaku Ananse could never place his hands on Mensisi again. Also, he had to take a live goat so that they could go to forest and ask for the ancestors to intercede with Yaa Somu on his behalf. Oh, Kwaku, Kwaku! Would he listen? No. He said Yaa Somu was anyɛn who had taken his wife away from him and he wasn't going to beg her for anything.

So, it cannot be said that Kwaku Ananse wasn't given a chance to save himself. He was given counsel many times, and Mensisi herself always forgave him, but he never changed, he never listened.

Before you arrived (Kwadwo and Garba, I'm talking about you) a *policeman* came here; he was called *Sargie*. He was a good-looking man, but I couldn't decide if I liked him. Sometimes he was polite, and sometimes he was rude, and though we tried to welcome him, his men were very disrespectful to some of our elders. I still don't know if he was a good or bad man. Maybe this is the way it was with Kwaku Ananse. He was a very good man when he wanted to be, but most of the time he was bad. (Our *Kenyan* friend says even the Englishman first went to his land with gifts.) Now, if you consider Mensisi, you have to remember that her mother died when she was born and it was mainly her father who raised her. Maybe that's why she kept coming back; because, this story I am telling you is hard to believe when you think that she knew what her father could do to her but she kept coming back. Again, remember that I said when Mensisi's first child died in her womb her father's illness stopped. Sebi, what Oduro told me was that Yaa Somu's curse meant that every time Mensisi conceived, Kwaku Ananse would fall ill. And it is this same illness that always brought Mensisi back to him, because no child likes to see their father ill.

So we were here in '76 when she came again. This time Kwaku Ananse had gone to visit Mensisi in Kumasi. Because he was ill, James had taken him to the *hospital* but the doctors said they couldn't find his illness so he was probably tired. They advised him to rest as much as possible, but he said he couldn't rest in Kumasi, so, even though she was pregnant, Mensisi said she would go home with him so someone could cook for him. Her husband wasn't very happy but he agreed.

So in '76 she was here again. (This was the year we heard on the Akasanoma that the leader of the land, Acheampong, had put many people in prison because he said they were planning to destool him.) Within three nawotwe of her return, we witnessed Kwaku Ananse's madness again. This time, when Mensisi went to forest, I knew where she was going so I didn't follow her. That time James went to the *police* but, because of the problems with Acheampong, they said *national security* was their priority and small quarrels at home were not their concern. Our chief summoned Kwaku Ananse and counselled him to behave in ways better fitting a man. Kwaku Ananse seemed to take the chief's counsel and in '79, when James and Mensisi had to move to Accra because of a new job James had got there, Mensisi stayed for a whole moon and there was no matter. Mensisi didn't conceive that year, in fact she didn't conceive for more than four years after '76.

In '81 she conceived again in Accra and she came here in the first moon of '82 to stay for some time. There had just been a *coup* in Accra and James didn't want her to be there during the *curfews*, with all the *soldiers* around. This time he wasn't worried because after Mensisi stayed in '79, we were all convinced that Kwaku Ananse's madness had gone. More than that, I was there when Oduro counselled him again. This time he told him about the curse. He said it was an old curse – a woman's curse – from a time, hundreds of years before Yaa Asantewa, when the Asantehene's son travelled to Sudan and fell in love. (That is also another story.) But what Oduro told Kwaku Ananse was that if he laid his hands on Mensisi a third time, his fate would be out of the hands of the living; the ancestors would intervene and deliver their own justice, for everyone is allowed to make a mistake twice and ask for forgiveness. But if you do the same thing three times, you are insulting the wisdom of all who came before you.

So we didn't think Kwaku Ananse would raise his hand again.

It wasn't long after Mensisi came that our chief summoned me. The leopard skin for his palace, which had been there since the time of his grandfather's father, had begun to tear.

He summoned me because in the days of our elders, when the chiefs took tributes to Asanteman, it was my family that used to go with his family to hunt so that we could pay our respects to Asanteman. The old laws allowed him to travel as far west as Bia to hunt a leopard every two years, but he did not know the new laws. Some of the hunting we did was now called *poaching* by those who had been educated by the Englishman. But the lands were still Asante lands and according to his family's pact with the Asantehene, the chief wanted a leopard. He summoned me because I know the ways of the rivers and forest, and can see my way through our forest without being seen; I was to travel as far as Bia to bring him a leopard.

Garba raised his hand to interrupt the hunter. 'Can you still catch leopards?' He was fascinated.

'Yes.'

'I mean, even today? In Ghana?'

The hunter nodded. 'Maybe they have moved away from where I used to go, but they are there.'

'You know, my family trains horses and donkeys, but my ancestors used to have to travel as far north as Mali to find wild ones.'

Kayo frowned. 'Where do they get them now?'

'Oh, now it's all changed. The chiefs buy the horses from North African traders. As for the donkeys they have reproduced so much that we have enough in Upper East Region.'

Kayo laughed.

The hunter coughed. 'Young men, can I finish my story?'

'Sorry,' said Garba. 'Carry on.'

So, when Mensisi came in '82, it wasn't two nights before I made the road to seek the chief's leopard. I took my cutlass, knives and my long gun and went through forest towards our mountains to join our river Birim. There, I felled two palms, joined them with hamabiri and cut a long stick to guide my way on the river. It is true that we have roads in this land, but when you know the ways of the river, that is how to move in forest. The ways of the rivers, their beauty is so much more than the ways of the roads. By the river you see the sukooko, nkwantabisa with its flowers like blood, chameleons, cuckoos, aburuburu, parrots and guineafowl. Guineafowl are why I am never hungry when I make the road. If I catch one and prepare it, I can eat its flesh for two days. I let the Birim water carry me down to the place where it meets the Pra and Ofin, near Dunkwa. There I stayed close to the bank so I could use my long stick to fight the water's current (otherwise the rivers would take me to the sea near Komenda). When I came out of the water near Dunkwa, I had done a day's travel. The darkness had not yet come, but it was late so I readied myself for the night, to rest and prepare to fight the river Ofin. The night is black black in forest and to get to the place where I could see the mountains at Aya I had to travel upstream. So in the morning, I went up the river Ofin and when I saw the mountains at Aya I got out of the water. I hid the palm trunks I was travelling on amongst some young trees and walked to the river Tano. (I was glad I was in forest because the sun had come.) It was a lot of walking so I was happy that there was abundant fruit. Just above Goaso, the river Tano is narrow; that is where I crossed. I rested there then made the road to the river Bia and crossed it also, in the Asuanta area. When you get to forest at Asuanta you are already close to leopards so you have to be alert. Onyame knows, that's why he put kola trees in that area. Evening had come when I reached Asuanta so I found a place to settle, chewed some kola and stayed up. Leopards are not easy to find, but it is important to watch them before you kill any. It is not good to kill the young ones or the females, and the males, you have to look well; if you kill one that is with a female that has new children, another male will come to claim her and kill the children. You want the adult male, but the less mature ones, their skin is also nicer. In our young days, we didn't have to go to Bia to find leopards; there were some just here until they started building the roads. (This James, Mensisi's husband, he was one of those building roads.) So I was in forest near Asuanta and Bia for three nights. On the third morning, just when the darkness was going, I heard some duiker near a stream, and I knew one of the leopards I was tracking was close, so I stayed in the bushes and watched them. It was as though I knew; it wasn't long before the leopard came. It was a fine leopard, with shiny skin, like a swamp viper. As it crouched, I raised my long gun and shot it between the eyes before it could pounce. The duiker ran in all directions and the birds took off like little messengers. I went to the beast with my knife to skin it, and cut the hind legs for the chief. I also took the forelegs to celebrate at home.

If you add all the days, I was gone for nawotwe. When I returned, Mensisi was gone. Kwaku Ananse was sitting in front of his home; he was talking to nobody. It was Oduro who told me that Kwaku Ananse had beaten Mensisi again. I couldn't believe it, but it is true that Mensisi was no longer there, so I asked if, sɛbi, the child she was carrying was OK. Oduro shook his head, and there, I cried. A grown person like me. I cried, because I couldn't understand what was wrong with Kwaku Ananse, killing his own grandchildren. I remembered what the women said when Mensisi was a girl, that Kwaku Ananse's love for his child was not natural, and I thought about the way the mature male leopards can kill baby leopards. I mean, I have spent my life in forest tracking animals, watching them.

All kinds of animals: birds, hogs, otwe, leopards, elephants, ndanko, snakes . . . I have seen them all with their children and none amongst them treats their offspring the way Kwaku Ananse treated his. A beast understands that when it is given power it must protect its young, those that depend on it. In my head I said, Onyame, the world is wondrous, and I have seen a lot of the beautiful wonders but this thing with Kwaku Ananse is one of the most terrible. How could the man sleep?

What the ancestors can do is beyond us. That is why it is better to honour them and not invoke their wrath. But this is precisely what Kwaku Ananse did. After Mensisi lost that third child, we knew, from what Oduro had said, that something would happen some day. So we waited.

In the first year we watched for signs but saw none. The palm wine tasted the same; the birds never stopped their singing; and my older son in Accra, with Onyame's generosity, had a child with one of his mother's people. Even Kwaku Ananse had the luck of a good man – a good harvest. The second year, '83, things did not seem much different and Kwaku Ananse began to think that the ancestors had taken their eyes off him. He became his old self, drinking strong palm wine and picking quarrels. As for me, I was seeing things in forest which made me wonder if all was well: the otwe and duiker were moving deep deep into forest because the water at Afema, the one that leads to the river Densu, was dry; even the river Bompom, just by Tafo, was not flowing with energy. Before long, the chief summoned us and told us that his linguist had heard on the Akasanoma – the *radio* – that there was a drought in our land, rain had not been falling well. And there we realised what was different. There had been no rain.

It is true that we still had crops but our harvest was light, there was not much left over for the farmers and traders to sell. As for Kwaku Ananse, sɛbi, his crop was destroyed that year, the cocoa pods that grew looked like a baby's fists, he could not sell them. I told my wife that the ancestors had started.

Mensisi came to visit her father during that time. James refused to get down from the car and greet Kwaku Ananse, but Mensisi (it seems she had started going to one of these *Pentecostal* churches) went to her father and embraced him. She said she had prayed for him and forgiven him. It was she who told us that, in the city, they were struggling for food and that more than one million of our people had been sent home from Alata.

Ei! Is it true? I said.

Mensisi, who was standing by the door of James' car preparing to leave, nodded. Egya, if you look in the *papers* you will see the *photos*. The way they pack them into *lorries*; they look like bread that is rising.

So this is how things carried on into '84, with everybody struggling to make life a little better. Even Gaw . . . our *Kenyan* friend said that these were trying times. As for Kwaku Ananse, because Mensisi had forgiven him, he started visiting Accra more frequently because there was no joy for him here. Sometimes he even brought things from my sons; it was Kwaku Ananse who brought my *radio* in '85, just a few months before Mensisi returned.

Kwaku Ananse had been sick with his coughing again, but Mensisi wasn't able to come and look after him because her husband was hurt. He had been in a bad *accident* while travelling to Takoradi to work and, sɛbi, they had to remove his leg. He was in bed for three moons but still things didn't get better and, with the passing of time, Onyame in his wisdom removed him from his suffering. The thing was, Mensisi was also with child, and James didn't want her to come to the village, but when he died, she was so sad alone in their home in Accra, and she knew her father was sick, so she came. She left the house in Accra with her mother's sisters to *rent* for her and she came back with the mind to stay.

When she came, we saw that the pregnancy had gone forward and she would deliver in less than four moons. Those of us who knew Kwaku Ananse were afraid for her; several of our women went to offer her a place to stay, but she said her father was sick so she would stay with him and care for him. I told you the girl had a mind of her own from when she was very young, not so? Hmm. We kept quiet and allowed her to do what she wanted, but we, the men, we watched Kwaku Ananse's home. We were ready, sɛbi, to kill him this time, if he started beating her again. We were ready because Kwaku Ananse to us was no longer a man, and, sɛbi, nobody mourns a tsetse fly when it dies.

So we watched Kwaku Ananse's home as though we were warriors; I would watch, then Tintin, then our friend from *Kenya* . . . Oduro told us that there was no need to watch, but we didn't believe him.

We were at our somewhere when it happened. I was the one on watch, but it was early evening so everybody was around. First we heard Kwaku Ananse raise his voice, so I took my long gun and went closer to his home. Then we heard Mensisi scream so I ran to the door of Kwaku Ananse's home, but before I could get there, we saw a boy come from forest; he was already as tall as me and muscular. He ran into Kwaku Ananse's home just before I got to the door. I would have gone inside also because the boy was not from our village, but I had seen something so I waited outside and listened. It remained quiet inside Kwaku Ananse's home so I went to Oduro to tell him what I had seen.

You see, they say, sɛbi, when something you don't know is approaching it is frightening, but when it gets close it is often a relative. It was that way with the boy; the way he bounded to Kwaku Ananse's door like a beast, I was fearful, but when he ran past me into the home I knew that there was no need to fear. Would you believe that the only cloth that the boy was wearing, a small piece around his waist, was the same cloth that I had seen Mensisi tearing twelve years before to cover her dead baby? Ei, this earth! I had seen ghost people before but not like this.

When I told Oduro he said, There you are. The ancestors are at work, the final part of the curse has begun.

I said, What will happen?

Oduro poured some palm wine into a calabash, and some onto the floor. The child will be born; it will be a girl.

And the boy?

He will be stronger than any man we have known; he will protect his mother. The rest will also come; the two left. They will come from forest like this one.

And there Oduro told me the whole matter. The boys had been sent back to Mensisi because her love for them was so strong. The other two would appear after this first one, in the order that they were meant to be born, and they would live amongst us and be helpers to their mother. They would be strong, but they would not be able to father children and they would die one year after their mother died.

Kwaku Ananse's punishment was that he was to grow younger but keep his adult mind so that he would understand what it is like to be at the mercy of someone else. He would lose twelve years when each boy arrived, and he would begin to lose weight. At first, when it started, Kwaku Ananse didn't know what it was. But he thought it was funny that he looked a little younger. He started following women again (in other villages, because the ones in K Krom didn't respect him) and began to think he would live forever. It was only when the third boy came and he really started to become thin that he realised the curse Yaa Somu had put on him was serious. He began to stay in his home; he became like a ghost in K Krom – sometimes you would see him sneaking off to his farm, but most of the time he was inside.

Ei! You would think that the punishment was finished, but there was more. Yaa Somu's curse was linked to Mensisi's first conception, so although her child was born more than twelve years later, that punishment was still there. We watched this girl grow up with her brothers (by this time, after the third boy came, Mensisi had left Kwaku Ananse's home and was living in Yaa Somu's home) and we didn't think anything of it. She would run around when her mother, Mensisi, was working with her brothers and we all laughed at the trouble she caused, forgetting that she was someone's punishment. Sɛbi, Oduro had forbidden the child from leaving the village until she was twenty years old, but we had all forgotten. I mean, we, the elders, knew, but we had forgotten. Is this not our problem as men? That we keep forgetting?

The hunter sat up and took the last piece of meat from his bowl. 'Hmm. What more is there to say? That is the story. Like all stories, it is a story about forgetting, for if we didn't forget there would be no mistakes and there would be no stories.'

Kayo fixed his eyes on Opanyin Poku, who had placed his arm over Mama Aku's shoulders, unsure of what to say. He scooped up the remnants of his palaver sauce with his fingers and licked them clean of the spicy, sweet palm oil.

'So the musician didn't see the babies growing?' Garba was still fixated on the giant xylophone, and all five of them – including Opanyin Poku – looked dazed with their empty bowls of food in front of them, and half-full calabashes balanced at odd angles.

Opanyin Poku laughed. 'The babies didn't grow. They just came as boys.'

Oduro and Mama Aku stared at Kayo; Mama Aku with a smile, Oduro with an intense concentration that would have scared Kayo if he wasn't so preoccupied.

'But they were good dancers, am I lying?' Garba persisted. 'Because they were put inside the heart of the music tree.'

'They were good dancers.' The hunter nodded at Garba. 'Very good dancers.'

Kayo held up his hand. The palm wine was making his head spin, but he was sure he had an opportunity to dig deeper. 'The cocoa farmer in your story, Kwaku Ananse, his daughter left him like Kofi Atta's daughter left him.'

'Yes, his daughter also left him.' The hunter nodded.

'But you know who the daughter is.'

'Yes, Mensisi.' The hunter held out his hand. 'I told you in the story.'

'It's true. He told us.' Garba confirmed.

Kayo shook his head as only a drunk man can. 'No, no, no. I mean, you know who Kofi Atta's daughter is.'

Mama Aku, who like Oduro had been silent, laughed. 'Oh, but we all know who Kofi Atta's daughter is. We all know each other in the village.'

Kayo shook his head again, more alert now. 'No, no, no, I mean . . .' He looked at Opanyin Poku and pointed. 'You know where she is because Kofi Atta is your relative.'

A palpable silence consumed the table. In the midst of all the voices at Akosua Darko's, it was like a sudden drop in pressure, significant enough to make heads turn and then turn back when they found no spectacle. Kayo knew he had struck a nerve. It was the piece of information he was least sure of, based on the assumption that whatever was in the hut was related to Kofi Atta, but it had made an impact.

Opanyin Poku raised his calabash and drank, but his hands were shaking. 'Did I tell you that?'

'No, but I know.' Kayo placed his hands, palms down, on the table. 'I know it's true.'

Garba turned to look at Kayo, his eyes alight with realisation. Kayo shook his head almost imperceptibly and Garba nodded.

'Well,' Opanyin Poku pulled his wife close. 'He is my relative.'

'So, did he beat his daughter? Is that why she left?' Kayo pushed for more, hoping he could confirm his suspicions.

Oduro, Opanyin Poku and Mama Aku all nodded.

'The way he beat her, it wasn't good at all,' Mama Aku added. 'It wasn't good.'

Kayo leaned forward now, closing the distance between himself and the hunter. His mind was racing. 'So, the story you just told us. Is it true? Is that the story of Kofi Atta?'

The hunter sighed. 'That may be your story. I am not the one to tell you what is true. I am telling you a story. On this earth, we have to choose the story we tell, because it affects us – it affects how we live.'

Garba tapped an Adowa beat on the side of his empty calabash then stopped. 'If I can speak . . .' He looked at Kayo, who nodded. 'Elders, you are making us dance. When we ask the questions, you give us a proverb. As for me, this is what I have to say. Yes, I am a policeman, but I don't want to bring trouble here. You are good people, you are good people . . .' Garba held up his hand as if to stop anyone else speaking while he caught his breath. 'We want to help you. My friend Mr Kayo, who is sitting here, maybe he doesn't know, but our senior policeman is crazy. If we don't tell him something, your village will never know peace again. I swear my mother, there will be policemen here until, excuse me to say, you all die. So, you choose the story you want to tell.'

There was another long silence then Oduro spoke. 'You cannot speak of what you have seen or heard here.'

Kayo frowned. 'Why?'

'When I sent you to go and burn that thing in the bamboo, the smoke that you inhaled was a spell. If you speak of anything you have seen or heard here to anyone outside this village, it will sound as though you are crying.'

'If that is the case, why can't you just tell us the truth?' Kayo surprised himself by slapping his palm on the table.

Oduro smiled. 'Patience.' He put his hand on Kayo's. 'It is not the right time.'

Kayo could feel control of his investigation shifting back to the secretive core of the village. He had with him the people who knew the most and there was no way, he decided, no way, he was going to sleep that night without knowing the truth about the remains. 'I have heard everything, but I also know something else. The thing in Kofi Atta's hut, it is from Akosua Darko's son or her father. I can go and ask her about it, or you can tell me what it is.' He turned to Oduro on his right. 'Egya Oduro, do you know?'

Oduro nodded and looked at Opanyin Poku who pulled his wife even closer. The hunter stared at Kayo, and, for the first time, Kayo noticed the brown flecks in the whites of his eyes. He looked like an old man, not the wiry, wily hunter Kayo had seen him as.

'Kwadwo . . .' Opanyin Poku paused and put his right hand on his face.

Mama Aku rubbed the hunter's back. 'Yaw, it's OK, it's OK.'

The hunter removed his hand and lifted his chin. 'It is her father. Kofi Atta was Akosua Darko's father. He beat her. He beat her . . .' He put his hand back on his face.

Kayo watched Mama Aku's shadow merge with the hunter's

on the wall behind them, then looked down at the dark shape of his own hand on the table.

Oduro sighed, and Garba said, 'Listen.'

In the distance was the clear sound of a xylophone, a song of fallen trees.

menada

KAYO STOOD IN THE MIDDLE OF KOFI ATTA'S HUT LOOKING OUT of the window-hole into the forest. He had spent the night reviewing the evidence collected at the crime scene, trying to put together a coherent hypothesis, something that would stand the scrutiny of other officers. There was no way, to his mind, he would have a full outline of what happened in Kofi Atta's hut by the end of the week. Indeed, he was beginning to think that the real truth, like love, was beyond the reach of scientific explication; and, as much as that irked him, he was also aware that Inspector P. J. Donkor had wanted a report at the end of the day, which Kayo had provided. All that was needed now was to ensure that any testimonies the villagers might give would mesh with the report. To his advantage, he knew there were no highly specialised forensic personnel with the Ghana Police, and more importantly the remains had been destroyed to appease the chief.

Looking back, Kayo wondered if the moment he had agreed to Nana Sekyere's request to let Oduro specify the mode of disposal of the remains was the moment that this had stopped being a scientific case. Yet who was he to come to their village, dispense with their traditions and etiquette, and throw their world into disarray with a science that still left you guessing?

Kayo sighed and pushed his hands into his pockets. Now that he had been in the village for three consecutive days he was asking himself the same questions the hunter had asked him on the first day they had met, when they were walking to the chief's palace.

'So, Kwadwo, are you a policeman?'

'No, Opanyin, I am only helping them. My job is to explain crimes. Death and things like that.'

The hunter threw his head back and laughed so hard that Mensah and Garba, who were walking ahead of them, stopped for a moment before they continued. Opanyin Poku pointed at Kayo. 'You explain deaths?'

'Yes.' Kayo's tone was defiant.

'Then, tell me, why do people die?'

'Because they are old, or sick, or someone attacks them. I don't know.'

'Then you can't explain deaths.'

'Opanyin, that is my job. It is part of what I do.'

'I am also a hunter. I kill beasts so I can eat, but I know that they don't die because I shoot them or trap them; that is how they die but that is not why they die. Why do some beasts escape the traps, and some get caught, eh? I mean an antelope that has been in forest its whole life, why does it come in front of my long gun on one particular day? Can you tell me?'

'No. Maybe luck?'

The hunter shook his head. 'Anyone who believes in luck doesn't know the power of Onyame or the ancestors.'

The hunter was right; there was no 'why' in his job. You could go as far as finding a motive for a murder, and the specific method for the murder, but you couldn't say why the victim died at 6:03 a.m. instead of 6:02 a.m.; there was always an unknown. His grandfather, Okaikwei, had died in shallow water, but no matter how much he queried it, he would never find out why. According to the 'wise ones' – as Opanyin Poku would say – that is for the ancestors to know. Kayo chuckled. It bemused him how the hunter could be fascinated by his profession and the gadgets he used, even reservedly respect some of the work he did, and yet be disdainful of it. But maybe that was the way to be; maybe he'd be better equipped to understand life if he didn't believe in absolute truths.

Kayo looked at his watch; it was 11:14 a.m. Garba would be back from Koforidua soon and Kayo was sure that within twenty-four hours Inspector Donkor would arrive. He needed to speak to Opanyin Poku. He turned and walked out of Kofi Atta's hut.

'Agoo.' Kayo stood a few metres away from the door to the hunter's hut.

'Amɛɛ.' Mama Aku's voice sang above the constant rustle of leaves that was Sonokrom's chorus.

'Kwadwo, is that you?' Opanyin Poku sounded as though his mouth was full.

'Yes, Opanyin, it is I.'

'Oh, come, come.' Opanyin Poku lifted the mat covering the door and waved Kayo in.

Mama Aku's and Opanyin Poku's hut had three window-holes instead of the usual one, so even with the doorway covered, there was plenty of light. The hunter's radio stood on the edge of the table from which Mama Aku rose, blaring out a song Kayo did not recognise. Mama Aku placed a stool in front of the table. On the table was a small mortar of freshly ground red pepper, some fried tilapia and kenkey.

Mama Aku brought a bowl of fresh water. 'You have come to meet us. Please wash your hands and join us.'

Kayo grinned and washed his hands. He hadn't smelled fish since he left Accra two days ago. According to tradition, he couldn't really refuse, but he didn't even want to.

The hunter and his wife waited for Kayo to finish washing his hands.

'You see,' said the hunter, 'I hunt meat but every Saturday this woman makes me go and catch tilapia for her.'

Kayo already had his first morsel of kenkey in his mouth and was breaking off a piece of fish so he just nodded.

'Don't mind him,' Mama Aku retorted. 'When he came to chase me in Accra I told him I wouldn't go with him unless he could promise me fish. I didn't force him.'

Kayo smiled. 'You know, my mother sells fish. I'll have some sent to you. I'm sure you haven't eaten sea fish in a while.'

'Oh Kwadwo, the way sometimes I crave fresh maŋ and tsile.'

The hunter watched Kayo with a wide grin on his face. 'You this Accra boy. You are coming to give my wife dreams of leaving.'

Mama Aku laughed. 'Oh, get away. Who would want me now that you've finished using me?'

Kayo almost choked as he joined in the laughter. He coughed to clear his throat and the hunter rose to get him a calabash of water.

'Pour some on the ground,' Opanyin Poku said after Kayo had stopped coughing. 'The ancestors have been kind to you, let them have some water.'

Kayo poured a few drops on the clay floor, then nodded at Opanyin Poku. 'I need to speak to you about police matters.'

Opanyin Poku looked at his wife. 'We are listening.'

'I don't know if the police will ask you any more questions, but if they do, tell them what you told me: that you are his cousin, he had no friends and his daughter had left him. But . . .' Kayo paused. 'I also want you to tell them that he had a woman in Côte d'Ivoire who used to come here sometimes.'

'Kofi Atta?' Mama Aku whispered.

'Yes.'

Opanyin Poku nodded. 'Carry on.'

'A few weeks ago, some men from Côte d'Ivoire, carrying matchets, came looking for Kofi Atta. They said they had come to warn him for beating their relative while she was pregnant, and, after that, you never saw them again. That's it.'

Opanyin Poku stood up. 'I have heard. Am I the only one to know this story?'

Kayo shook his head while washing his hands in the bowl on the table. 'I have told you so that you can let the story get to those who need to know.' Kayo stood up to leave.

The hunter stepped forward and took Kayo's hand. 'Kwadwo, you have honoured our ways.'

Kayo shook his head. 'Mama Aku, thank you for the food.'

Mama Aku walked over to hug Kayo. 'There is no thanks between us. You are my child.'

Kayo waited inside his hut until Garba returned from Koforidua. As soon as he heard the hum of the Range Rover engine, he jumped up from his mat and went to the doorway.

Garba was jogging up to the hut. 'Mission accomplished, sah.'

'You faxed the report? Are you sure it was received?'

Garba was still wearing mufti and he looked like a man who had lost his way as he grinned. 'Received and actioned. They radioed me on the way back. Donkor himself is coming.'

'Donkor?' Kayo had not anticipated such an early encounter with the inspector. 'How long does it take to drive here?'

'I think . . .' Garba scratched his now thick beard. 'In convoy, I think two and a half hours.'

'OK, Garba, read the report and remember the details. We have to be speaking the same language.'

'Yes sah.' Garba hesitated.

'Garba, where is the printout?'

'Oh,' Garba smiled sheepishly. 'It's in the car.' He crossed the space between the hut and the car in twelve great bounds and returned with the printout.

Kayo sat back on his mat and stretched into a reclining position. He closed his eyes and tried to relax.

'Mr Kayo.'

Kayo opened one eye and looked at Garba, who had pulled his mat close to Kayo's and was sitting facing him.

Garba held out the printed sheets to Kayo. 'Sah, can you read it to me? I remember easier that way – it's like a story.'

Kayo sighed, snatched the papers from Garba and sat up.

On Wednesday 21 July 2004, at approximately 9:45 a.m., following a lengthy discussion, I was assigned by the Police Regional Coordinating Chief, Inspector Percival Joseph Donkor, to provide scene of crime investigation services in Sonokrom, Eastern Region, at a suspected homicide scene. I was provided competent and experienced support in the person of Constable Garba Musah of the Greater Accra Police Force, who was instructed to drive me to the scene of crime.

The particulars of the case as I received them were as follows:

- *A male witness (A) and a female witness (B) had come upon what were suspected to be human remains in a hut in the hinterland and had reported to the authorities in Accra.*
- *A team of officers had been deployed to the village where preliminary investigations had been done.*
- *A pathologist, called in to analyse the remains, speculated that they were afterbirth, but was uncertain.*
- *It was decided, after deliberation at the highest level, that a scenes-of-crime expert must be called in, and I was thus appointed.*

On arrival at Sonokrom at 1:17 p.m., Constable Garba Musah and I were met by Detective Constable Isaiah Mensah who, after our consultation with the chief of Sonokrom, Nana Sekyere, led us to the scene of crime, which was a hut allegedly belonging to a Mr Kofi Barima Atta. We arrived at the scene at 1:56 p.m. The scene of crime was located to the far north-east corner of the village in close proximity to a hut belonging to the local palm-wine tapper, Mr Kwaku Owusu. A heap of charcoal and debris from a broken pot were found on the external periphery of the scene, and in the doorway a smooth, shiny, oval and black object was found, identified by DC Mensah as Bosomtwe stone, commonly used as a coolant in water pots. All the objects were photographed, tagged in numerical order and bagged for reference.

The interior was a circular space with clay walls and floors and no dividing walls. The contents of the room were: a pot of palm wine, three pieces of folded cloth, some decaying food, a table, an enamel plate and two cooking pots. All the items were processed by DC Mensah for fingerprints and the room was subjected to a 450 nanometre blue merge scan. The scan revealed apparent medium to high velocity-type spatter and drops of suspected urine. The velocity range suggested auto-emission or pouring. The flesh remains mentioned in the initial case report were located on a straw mat in the middle of the room. Close examination revealed the presence of housefly maggots in the remains, which were of indeterminate shape and foul-smelling. Fluid and tissue samples were taken from the flesh mass, and examples of the maggots were also taken. All flesh and fluid samples were frozen in liquid nitrogen and taken to Accra by DC Mensah for testing. The flesh remains were subsequently burned in the interest of public health, given their advanced state of putrefaction. Processing of the scene of crime was completed at 5:36 p.m.

On Friday 23 July 2004, Constable Garba Musah conducted thorough interviews with all the adults resident in Sonokrom. None of the persons interviewed had seen Kofi Atta for one moon (translated from Akuapem Twi as one month), however, the palm-wine tapper, Mr Kwaku Owusu, had heard a pot breaking in the hours before the morning when the remains were discovered by Witness A and Witness B. Further, Mr Yaw Onunum Poku, a hunter and cousin of Mr Kofi Barima Atta, revealed that a group of five men from Côte d'Ivoire had come looking for Mr Kofi Barima Atta some weeks prior to the discovery of the remains, and had exhibited threatening behaviour. They were carrying cutlasses, and said that they had come to warn Mr Kofi Barima Atta, who had a history of domestic violence, for beating their relative, who, allegedly, was Kofi Barima Atta's partner.

Garba shifted and scratched his beard.

Kayo looked up. 'Is there a problem?'

'No, sah, I believe it. I like the way you describe me, and I'm OK with the crime scene, but . . .' Garba smiled and scratched his beard again. 'Where from this woman too?'

'A dysfunctional affair; to give motive.' Kayo put the report to one side. 'You see, because of the trouble in Côte d'Ivoire no one can really check. The truth is, we still don't know how the remains got to the hut. But we need something.'

Garba nodded and tugged at a single hair on his chin. 'Oh, I see now. Diversion tactics.' He laughed. 'You be one-man-thousand true true!'

Kayo shook his head. 'Chale, you listen first, before Donkor arrives.' He picked up the report.

Laboratory results confirmed that the suspected urine and the fluid from the remains came from the same DNA source, and both samples shared x-chromosome traits with the DNA of Mr

Yaw Onunum Poku, whose mother was the older sister of Mr Kofi Barima Atta's mother. Further, it was concluded, based on tissue analysis, that the flesh remains had characteristics consistent with a human lung. This suggests that Mr Kofi Barima Atta is likely to be deceased.

It is thus my hypothesis that Mr Kofi Barima Atta was aware that the men from Côte d'Ivoire were looking for him. He thus went into hiding, but was found and murdered sometime between 30 June 2004, when the group of men from Côte d'Ivoire appeared in Sonokrom, and the morning of Sunday 18 July 2004, when the suspected lung was discovered. One of the men from Côte d'Ivoire then came back to Sonokrom between the night of Saturday 17 July 2004 and the morning of Sunday 18 July 2004, to deposit the lung in Mr Kofi Barima Atta's hut, and pour Mr Kofi Barima Atta's own urine at the scene of crime to desecrate his remains. In the haste to complete the dumping of the brutal remains, the perpetrator broke the water pot outside Mr Kofi Barima Atta's hut. This hypothesis is consistent with the laboratory findings and the splatter of the urine.

'Ei, sah, can't they check the sample?'

Kayo smiled. 'Don't worry, the lab man is my friend. Lung tissue is not hard to find and he's the only one who can do DNA reliably.' He stood up. 'Your boss self, e no dey mind the results. E want murder, so I give am murder. You go remember the details?'

'Oh, I go remember. E be fine story.'

Kayo hadn't expected the press to arrive with Inspector Donkor, but they did. They came in a convoy of two police jeeps, descended and fanned out like a disturbed trail of soldier ants.

Inspector Donkor himself emerged from the passenger side of a dark blue Range Rover, similar to the one Garba had secured for their return to Sonokrom, but with tinted windows. P. J. Donkor was in full ceremonial gear, with a white braid stark against the dark blue of his uniform. He smiled when he saw Kayo, walked towards him with brisk, short strides and shook his hand. There was a sudden series of flashes as four cameramen scrambled to get images of the inspector embracing Kayo.

'Well done,' the inspector whispered in Kayo's ear. 'The Côte d'Ivoire link is perfect, just perfect. A multinational case.'

'Thank you.' Kayo looked over the inspector's head to see the driver of the vehicle, a thickset man of medium height with silver reflective sunglasses, tipping his hat at Kayo.

The inspector turned. 'Ah, Odamtten, meet Sergeant Mintah, my most trusted right-hand man. A former army man.' He placed his hand on Kayo's lower back as though he wanted to push him towards Sergeant Mintah, then clicked his fingers at Garba. 'Constable, come and show me the scene.'

Kayo shook Sergeant Mintah's hand. 'Hello, sah.' He smiled at his own reflection in the sergeant's sunglasses. 'So you are the one who called me at work.' Stevie Wonder's mellifluous voice singing 'Don't You Worry 'Bout A Thing' at the end of that conversation rang through Kayo's mind.

Sergeant Mintah smiled, revealing a broken tooth in the upper front row. 'Guilty. I was looking forward to meeting you. I hear you gave the inspector a tough time.'

'I don't think so. I think he was playing with me.'

Sergeant Mintah's face hardened briefly. 'Make sure you remember that. He is a very particular man.' He reached into the car, took out a newspaper from the day before and showed it to Kayo.

Under a caption 'MURDER MYSTERY IN SONOKROM' was a picture of Kayo, laden with his laptop bag and forensics case, taken by Kakra when Kayo first arrived from England. The text beneath it read 'Ghanaian forensics expert from England steps in – more on page 3'.

Sergeant Mintah put the paper back in the car. 'The inspector issued a communiqué when you left Accra. Knowing him, I took your payment to your mother when I collected the picture. You should—'

'Sah,' Garba pulled up beside the two men, out of breath. 'Mr Kayo. Donkor says you should come and take a picture by Kofi Atta's hut.'

Kayo shook Sergeant Mintah's hand once more and followed Garba to Kofi Atta's hut.

Inspector Donkor was standing in the doorway with the hunter, who looked as if he had been transplanted there with his radio, unkempt beside the polished grooming of the inspector. Kayo and Garba joined them for some staged group photographs, then Inspector Donkor took two steps forward and cleared his throat. Two press men with video cameras jostled their way to the front of the assembled journalists and composed their shots.

Inspector Donkor's voice rang out, clear and deep. 'Countrymen, I have been with the Ghana Police Force for several years, working my way through the ranks, and I can not remember a prouder moment. Here we have a murder case, with international perpetrators, solved in record time, less than a week after it was reported. I want you to know that this is the new face of the Ghana Police Force – with the harnessing of high-level investigation, the best technology, and cross-continental expertise, no criminal is safe: not here, not in Koforidua, not in Accra, nowhere in Ghana . . . not even in Siberia.' The inspector took a white handkerchief out of his pocket and wiped the sweat forming on his forehead. 'Here we have a man who has been brutally murdered by the worst kind of cowards, those who can't even respect the dead, but, with our forensics expertise,

164

we have a watertight case against them, we know who they are.'
The inspector's cheek twitched twice. 'I'm telling you today –
DNA doesn't lie. According to our thorough investigations, they
have run away to Côte d'Ivoire, but we, your police, would like
you to know that we will uphold the reputation of our force,
and demonstrate our nation's leadership in international security; we will find them. We will go into the civil war and smoke
those rats out from their holes.' The inspector set his face into
a stern mask. 'For now, our thoughts must lie with the cousin
of the victim,' he gestured in the direction of Opanyin Poku,
'whose great loss this is. Thank you.'

In a moment of synchronised perfection, both cameras
panned to Opanyin Poku, who had a look of intense concentration, then back to Inspector Donkor's face for a final
close-up shot.

By the time Inspector P. J. Donkor had finished speaking, most
of the village had gathered to watch. He waved at them, then
grabbed Kayo by the hand and urged him towards Sergeant
Mintah and the Range Rover.

'So, my *CSI* man, your report was fantastic. The processing
of the, the, the . . .' The inspector's cheek twitched with the
effort of remembering. 'The evidence. The hypothesis . . . I
think you could be a valuable addition to the police force.'
Donkor smiled, revealing his tiny teeth for a fraction longer
than usual. 'Join us for a drink.'

Kayo looked towards Oduro's hut, beyond which was the
hut where his belongings were. 'OK, let me just get my laptop.'

Donkor grinned. 'No need. We'll radio Garba to take care
of it. Come.' He put his arm around Kayo's shoulder and
opened the back door of the Range Rover for him.

Sergeant Mintah settled in the driver's seat and started the
engine.

As soon as Inspector Donkor was seated, they pulled out and took to the road, heading away from Koforidua and Accra. The road's surface remained smooth, a grey plaster of modernity over the wound of nature.

When they had been driving for a couple of minutes, Inspector Donkor opened the glove compartment and took out a bottle of Jack Daniels and three shot glasses.

'The drink of Frank Sinatra,' the inspector said as he filled the glasses. He passed one to Kayo. 'It is only right to celebrate on the road that brought us our good fortune.' He knocked the drink back and slapped his chest.

Sergeant Mintah downed his with a silent efficiency.

Kayo waited for the two officers to finish before he gulped his. 'What do you mean?'

The inspector laughed. 'This is the road the minister built for his girlfriend, and now, because of her, I'm sure to move up two ranks. She was so relieved to hear the thing was just a lung. She was seeing a spiritualist. Now, three, four, more years and I will be head of Ghana Police.'

'Oh,' Kayo nodded.

'So how much of that report is true?' The inspector turned suddenly to fix his granite stare on Kayo.

'It's all true, Inspector.' Kayo twirled the empty glass between his fingers.

'It wouldn't be wise to lie to me.' Donkor's gaze didn't shift.

'It's all true.' Kayo held out his glass for a refill.

'Fine.' The inspector turned to face the road, leaving Kayo's arm aloft. 'Now we need to speak about your future. As we agreed, you will be head of new forensic techniques and you will be under the BNI. But you will report to me.' The inspector turned to Kayo, holding his hands in a triangle over his mouth. 'I need an inside man at the bureau.'

Kayo pondered his conversations with Garba, Sergeant

Ofosu's comments and his own experience in the past week, then shook his head. 'I haven't made up my mind about whether or not I want to work for the force.' As soon as he said it he knew he shouldn't have. An image of the dark shape beneath the chair at Donkor's house flashed through his mind and he remembered the embroidered sepow, an image from Kwesi Brew's poem 'The Executioner's Dream'. It was too late.

Inspector Donkor turned to face forward, looked at Kayo in the rear-view mirror, and smiled. He glanced at Sergeant Mintah. 'Sergeant, drive off road and park.'

Kayo checked his door; it was locked.

Mintah did as the inspector said, the glint of light in his sunglasses seeking Kayo in the back seat as he parked in a clearing.

Inspector Donkor unlocked Kayo's door and took his pistol out of its holster. 'Get down,' he ordered.

Kayo got out of the car and let Inspector Donkor lead him to a cassia tree, where Kayo turned to face him. In the distance, the sun glanced off Sergeant Mintah's glasses as though the man was winking at him.

'Listen,' the inspector spoke in the same voice he had used for his TV speech. 'I like you, and you are a smart man so I will give you one final chance. You know too much about the benefit of this case, so either you are with me or against me. If you are not working for me I will have to kill you to keep our common secrets sacred.' The inspector's cheek twitched three times. 'Listen, I can help you. You will never have to worry about money again and soon you will be rising through the ranks. Isn't that what you wanted?'

Kayo could feel the staccato of his heart in the pulse at his temple. He looked at Sergeant Mintah, who shook his head slowly. Saying yes would save Kayo's life, but it would make him P. J. Donkor's pawn; he hadn't worked all his life for that.

He could tell that there were no escape options; they were isolated. He had to bluff. Kayo looked the inspector in the eye. 'People would know you killed me. I was seen leaving the village with you.'

Inspector Donkor laughed. 'Do I look stupid? I didn't get to my position without learning to cover my tracks. Yes, I left with you, but your body will not be found for a few days.' The inspector lowered the pistol and smiled. 'You have just solved a major murder case, your picture is in the paper – front page; you are recognisable, you are a target, the murderers are at large. So, you decide.'

Kayo held the inspector's piercing gaze, knowing that, contrary to the training he had received, he was acting on instinct over logic. 'You might as well shoot me then.' He turned and walked towards the dark mass of the forest beyond the clearing. The last thing he saw as he turned was Inspector Donkor raising his pistol to take aim.

*

Ei, wonders will never cease. They say nothing is other than what you see, but it is also true that nothing is other than what you don't see. So, I was sitting on this same wood that lightning cut down on the day that Kofi Atta beat Akosua, and the *graduate*, this Kwadwo who is now with us three days a week as a *doctor* (I think he is learning something from Oduro), told me that the senior *policeman* tried to shoot him.

So I said, Really, he tried to shoot you?

And he said, Ehh, he raised his gun and pulled the *trigger*, but I think the other one, Mintah, had removed the *bullets*.

Hmm, can you believe that this Mintah, the one who removed the *bullets*, also took money to his mother for him? That's why the elders say that, sɛbi, bad doesn't live alone in a compound; good always lives there too.

But this senior *policeman*, he is trouble; when you look at him you think he is kind, but he laughed when he tried to shoot Kwadwo. He called him *stubborn man* and said he was *lucky* this time, but he would come and look for him another time. And Kwadwo was sitting here laughing about it. These young men! Thanks to Onyame's generosity, Kwadwo knew his way through forest to come back. (I told him he would be a good hunter, didn't I? I always say, in this land of ours, if you travel by forest or water, nobody can see you.)

Anyway, I told Kwadwo that this is why you have to look well with people because you never know their story. I mean, they say what happens for a woman to conceive – sɛbi, not the lying down, but what happens after – is a mystery to all men. But (this is what I told him), my friend, I tell you, what happens after birth is a bigger mystery. Something as unprofitable as an unburied umbilical cord can change history.

Did I tell you the story of our *Kenyan* friend, Gawana? I said to Kwadwo.

Opanyin, he said, I don't want a new story. I want the end of the story that you were telling us; Kofi Atta's story. I am going to Accra tomorrow and Garba will ask. It's already getting late.

Ei, you and your young hurry. Will you come for a drink? Esi is there ooh. I laughed because I have seen his eyes wandering over her. We are not old for nothing; we see things.

He shook his head. No, I want you to tell me the story.

So, with the darkness coming, and the bats hovering above us, on this same wood, I told him.

The wise ones say that sometimes when the wrong that is done is bigger than us, justice is taken from our hands because we cannot carry it, and, in our zeal to hold it aloft, we may injure ourselves or those around us. This is why Oduro had told us that we didn't need to keep watch over Mensisi; the ancestors were in control. You see, Mensisi's child was the real punishment, for as soon as the child reached the age of her mother's first conception, Kwaku Ananse would start to lose one year a day, and for the final day, he would lose that which he hurt others with – his hardness, his bones. All this meant that in just nineteen days, sɛbi, all that would be left of him would be water. Remember that I told you that his mind would remain? Eh heh. So, what was in it was that, Oduro said that Kwaku Ananse would not turn to water; it was shame that would kill him, because he was too proud. He said that a woman would see Kwaku Ananse when all that was left of him was red flesh – the colour of a woman's troubles – and the shame of being seen would kill him. After that happened, no one was to see Kwaku Ananse for three days, after which we could burn what was left of him.

It is true that, because this woman with the short short skirt and thin legs, sɛbi, knew certain people, the police were here with their guns before the three days could come, so it didn't happen exactly as Oduro said. But, if everything happened as he said, I wouldn't be sitting here on this tree that the lightning felled telling you this story, so we have to accept that the ancestors had a plan. What is in it that is important is that when Kwaku Ananse was burned (you were there), it smelled exactly like the medicine man said it would – sweet, like justice.